GW01398859

THE CLASH OF SHADOWS

SHADOWS

Shards of Shadow Book 4

Joseph R. Lallo

Heart Ally Books, LLC

The Clash of Shadows
Copyright © 2024 by Joseph R. Lallo

All rights reserved. No portion of this book may be reproduced in any form without written permission from the publisher or author, except as permitted by U.S. copyright law.

NO AI TRAINING: Without in any way limiting the author's exclusive rights under copyright, any use of this publication to "train" generative artificial intelligence (AI) technologies to generate text is expressly prohibited. The publisher reserves all rights to license uses of this work for generative AI training and development of machine learning language models.

Art commissioned by Joseph Lallo as chapter headings by viiStar.

Cover design: Deranged Doctor Designs

Published by:

Heart Ally Books, LLC
heartallybooks.com
26910 92nd Ave NW C5-406, Stanwood, WA 98292
Published on Camano Island, WA, USA

ISBN-13: 978-1-63107-071-6 (paperback)
ISBN-13: 978-1-63107-074-7 (epub)

10 9 8 7 6 5 4 3 2 1

Contents

CHAPTER 1

A lan anxiously glanced at the clock. He'd been having biweekly sessions with his therapist for a few months, though he still thought of Dr. Ling as his friend Jessie's therapist, who he happened to be seeing sometimes. He couldn't fault her, she'd done everything in her power to make him more comfortable. In the most glaring example of the concessions she'd made, the lights in the office were kept so dim it probably made it difficult for her to take notes. But still, Alan was anxious. And if the doctor could hear what Alan heard, she wouldn't have to ask why. For that matter, if the doctor could see what Alan could see, she'd probably be a bit more anxious herself. Because right now an inky silhouette of living shadow stretched across the floor between them, up the wall behind her, and onto the ceiling to peer down at her notebook. Squinted white eyes scanned the page, the sharp line of her mouth turned down in a disapproving scowl.

"She wrote 'evasive' again, and underlined it twice. Stop being evasive," Blot hissed.

Alan resisted the urge to glance at the Shade. For other people undergoing therapy, figuring out how to silence the voice in their head or to stop seeing things was probably their goal. Alan's primary focus had been to treat his steadily more debilitating levels of stress without letting the therapist know about the voice and vision that had been complicating his life for the better part of a year at this point.

"That's enough about your career for today," the therapist said. "How have things been going in your personal life?"

"Oh, you know. Pretty good. I've been hanging out with Jessie a lot more."

"That's good to hear. I think you would be well served by increasing your support structure. Have you been spending your visits at her house? At yours? In public?"

"What does she care? Don't tell her. She's being nosy. But also don't be evasive," Blot said. "Tell her that you're not going to tell her out of respect for Jessie's privacy. That way it's not *you* being evasive, it's—"

"Mostly her place," Alan said steadily.

"Good, good," the doctor said, nodding.

"Why is that good? Ask her why that's good," Blot said. "She always gets happy whenever you talk about doing things with Jessie. Maybe she is in cahoots with Jessie, hmm? Jessie started seeing her first, after all."

"How do you spend your time, when the two of you are together?" the therapist asked.

"Specifically?" he asked.

"As specific or general as you like."

"Tell her you volunteer at a soup kitchen," Blot said. "No... wait... Jessie talks to her too. We need to find out what Jessie says so we don't contradict it. Tell her—"

"We've taken a mutual interest in some ongoing projects," Alan said.

A few days earlier...

Alan's and Jessie's peculiar schedules at the police station meant about once a week they completed their shifts at the same time. Over the course of a few weeks, a routine had developed where they would head back to her apartment at the end of the day. It was always ostensibly to unwind but seldom took long to devolve into one or more of three activities. One was discussing what was to be done about the Shades, the Glints, and everything else that the rest of the world was blissfully unaware of. One was allowing Blot to indulge in one of her burgeoning hobbies. And one was for Jessie and Blot to swap notes on the newest additions to their growing circles.

Today, it was all three.

"Okay, Frightful... you know what to do..." Jessie said, gazing at the shadow stretched across the floor at her feet.

The black form gazed up at her, one white eye unblinking. The figure was broadly that of a bird, though according to Blot it was more accurately called a rikt. Judging its size from the shadow was tricky, as it was distorted by the light that cast it. But in comparison to her own shadow, it was quite large, approaching that of an eagle's. Its head was cocked and hunched a bit. A poof of feathers rendered its outline ragged and fuzzy. Jessie held out her arm like a falconer and pointed at the coatrack beside the door.

"Go!" she said with authority in her voice.

Frightful hesitated in a way that suggested it was less out of fear or confusion and more out of a desire to make it clear she wasn't eager in her obedience. Then she coiled herself and hopped free of Jessie's arm. Jessie's eyeline quickly became inaccurate as Frightful reduced herself to an adorable little ribbon of a sprite, flitting about the walls, jumping from picture frame to picture frame, causing them to rock.

"Is she doing it?" Jessie asked, eyes darting to catch the phantom motions a moment after each happened.

Because Jessie lacked a Shade of her own, she could only see Blot and those of her world when Frightful was perched upon her. It made measuring the success of any bit of training that sent Frightful on her way a bit of a collaborative effort between herself and Alan.

"If she is, she's taking the long way around," Alan said, eyes on the sprite as it looped across to jostle the salt and pepper shakers individually.

"Frightful, if you want treats, you have to do the trick," Jessie said firmly.

The bowl of potpourri on the entry table wobbled in place as Frightful coiled into its shadow. Then, after a calculated delay, the rikt burst from the bowl and wrapped around the shadow of the coatrack.

Jessie saw the motion and stifled a gleeful squeal. She cleared her throat and held her arm out again, keeping it perfectly still. "... Well?" she asked after a moment.

"Still hiding behind the coatrack," Alan said.

"She's never going to do it," Blot muttered from the other room.

"I imagine Blot is making snide comments right about now," Jessie said, arm held firm.

Frightful's clutch was necessary for Jessie to actually *see* Blot and those like her, but her intuition had always been sharper than her vision.

Blot's form darted into the room and glared at Jessie, then at Alan. "Don't you dare tell her she's right," she said.

"No comment," Alan said.

"I thought so," Jessie said with a wry grin.

"It was a lucky guess. I'm not *that* predictable," Blot said, drifting back into the kitchen.

Jessie slapped her arm. "Come," she said.

Another pause, this one seemingly calculated to the fraction of a second to appear as though the command had been ignored. Then the coatrack rattled in place and the sprite launched toward her, swirling back to full size and alighting on the shadow of her arm. After a brief wince, a giggle of excitement burst from Jessie.

"Such a good girl! Such a good girl, Frightful!" she said, reaching into her pocket to produce a handful of kibble.

The shadow creature pecked at the shadow of the kibble, and bit by bit it vanished. Once the treat was delivered, Jessie eyed her shadow and guided her hand as near to the rikt's head as she could manage. It glared at her hand with its unblinking white eye, then leaned toward her and rubbed its ruffling feathers on the offered shadow.

"I wish I could feel it. I bet she's so fluffy..." Jessie said. "As it is, all I can feel is when her claws sink in. And I sort of wish I didn't."

"It beats the alternative," Alan said.

"And just what's that supposed to mean?" Blot shouted from the kitchen.

"Not that these last few months haven't been delightful, Blot, but I think you'll agree that from the human perspective having a tingly sensation in your arm is a less disruptive way to gain insight into the world of Shades than having your shadow torn off."

"I try not to see things from the human perspective. Dinner's almost done. What kind of cheese does everyone want? She has Pepper Jack and American," Blot said.

"Pepper Jack," Alan and Jessie said at the same time.

Alan craned his neck to see what was going on in the kitchen. Of all the utterly bizarre things that had happened since Blot entered his life, her growing interest in cooking might have been the most inexplicable. And that was an achievement, considering the list also contained fighting a shape-shifting drunk and doing business with beings that may or may not have been angels. If one didn't know to watch the shadows, it would have looked like the house was haunted. Slices of bread rose into the air to be smeared with mayonnaise and mustard. They plopped down on the skillet and were layered with cheese. As they sizzled and spat, the spoon in the simmering pot behind them rattled and stirred. Before long, a pair of grilled cheese sandwiches lifted off the skillet and onto plates. Cabinets opened and shut until the bowls could be found. Blot ladled them full of steaming soup, then splashed something into a second frying pan, causing a rush of steam.

"Have you tried training Chu-chu at all?" Jessie asked.

"Chu-chu is *my* pet, not his," Blot said. "Supper's done."

Alan and Jessie stood, marching out into the kitchen.

"Grilled cheese, homemade tomato soup, and..." Blot set down ramekins and drizzled them full of drippings from the pan. "Red-eye gravy."

"You're spoiling us, Blot. This is truly appreciated," Jessie said, sitting down and breathing in a savory whiff of the steaming soup.

"I figure if I do a good enough job in *your* kitchen, maybe Alan will quit being so stingy with the kitchen utensils at home," Blot said.

The shadow poured out a cup of coffee for herself from a French press, then flitted over to linger beside Alan. "Chu-chu!" she trilled.

The garbage bin beside the counter rattled and rustled, then a sprite whisked out and swirled to nestle into the shadow of the napkin holder. He peered out and accepted some pats and scratches from Blot far more readily than Frightful had.

"You don't think maybe you'd get some value from teaching him some commands?" Jessie said.

"He already knows everything he needs to know." Blot turned to the inky companion. "Isn't that right, Chu-chu?"

The smaller rikt tipped its head, then hacked. Something wet and gnawed-upon emerged into reality and flew across the room into the garbage can.

"Was that part of a shoe?" Alan asked.

"Yep! And he got it *right* in the garbage can," Blot said proudly. "That's a good Chu-chu. Have some bacon, Chu-chu."

Blot plucked a raw strip of bacon from the counter and tossed it in the air. It hung above the table as Chu-chu caught one end and Frightful caught the other, then split and vanished as they ate their share.

"You didn't earn that," Blot said, glaring at Frightful.

The larger rikt seemed unconcerned.

"Why is there raw bacon?" Alan said.

"For treats! And because I fried the rest up for the drippings for the gravy."

"Where'd the fried bacon go?" Jessie peered at the bowl. "Did you crumble it up into the soup?"

"Yes. They do it with pea soup, and I thought, why not?" Blot said. "Now eat, we have work to do before we call it a night. I think I'm almost done with the spell."

Though the bulk of the time during these evening visits had been spent kibitzing and playing with/training the rikts, ostensibly the true purpose was a much more important one.

Their last adventure had put Alan and Blot in touch with an elderly woman named Gladys, who had a Shade of her own. The two of them were simultaneously the wisest and least hostile host and Shade that Alan had encountered. They weren't strictly altruistic, though. Their lessons came at a price, mostly in the form of information and resources. But in exchange, Blot had earned a great deal of the education she probably should have gotten before she'd come to this world. She was learning magic, and though she was exceedingly amateur at the moment, she was thrilled to finally be building herself into something more than her superiors had intended her to be.

The first official spell she'd been taught was a stealth spell of sorts, one of a wide variety of spells that would prevent other magic-users from tracking or spying upon herself and Alan. The actual mechanism of the spell required things Alan couldn't begin to understand, but if the relative peace and safety of the weeks since they'd learned it were any indication, it was highly effective. However, that spell was the result of direct tutorial, and was designed specifically for Alan and Blot. In order to offer Jessie and others in Alan's circle a similar level of protection, it would have to be adapted. Blot had been fully committed to the task, slow though the progress had been.

"I'm *sure* I've got the spell figured out," she said, flicking a stack of pages into reality and leafing through them. "I won't bore you with stuff you won't understand. But the tricky bits were here and here. These shapes here on the paper? On the spell I was taught, they were completely different. They're the target part of the spell. I couldn't just make another copy of the spell I'd been given and cast it in the same way, because it'd just be protecting me and Alan again. I had to change it to protect Jessie and Frightful."

"That looked like just one word though. How can just one word refer to specifically you and Alan?" Jessie asked.

"Shows what you know," Blot said. "It's not a *word*. It's a *compound runic confluence*. A collection of shapes, which, when combined, carries a much more complex and specific meaning than its individual components."

Alan paused. "That sounds like a word."

"Well it's different," Blot said simply.

"Different how?" Jessie said.

"It just is," Blot snapped. "Do you have the thing?"

"The silver pendant?" Jessie asked. "It's in the box under my bed. I'll get it." She got up, having not had a chance to sample her meal, and trotted off to the bedroom.

"You're being a little abrasive, don't you think?" Alan whispered.

"Yeah, well, she's being a little nosy," Blot said.

"She's trying to educate herself. Ever since college, that's how she deals with things when they are feeling out of control for her. She finds the protocol and sticks to it. It's probably why she became a cop. Tons of protocol."

"Here it is!" Jessie said, marching out of the bedroom.

She held up a silver pendant. It had seen better days and was heavily tarnished and pitted like it had been dragged through gravel. The pendant was standard equipment for members of the Dawn, a group dedicated to the defeat of Shades like Blot. Alan and Blot had gotten it from Gladys in order to serve as a troubleshooting aid in Blot's quest to learn stealth magic. Since it came from a Shade-bearer, there was likely a *very* good reason for its poor state of repair. But it still served its purpose, because the angular piece had a clear and defined front, and presently that front was facing Blot regardless of how she or the hand holding the pendant moved.

"Should it be pointing at you?" Jessie said. "I thought you were hiding."

"The stealth doesn't work flawlessly at close range unless we're shadow diving. So let's test that part first."

"Better now than *after* dinner," Alan said, pushing his chair back. "I get the feeling if we did that on a full stomach, I might lose my lunch afterward."

"I'll make it quick," Blot said.

Blot slid up behind Alan. She eased her hands up out of the shadow, clutching him under his arms. With a sharp, sudden tug, she yanked him into the shadows with her. Alan had lost count of how many times he'd experienced this, but he'd yet to get comfortable with it. Sliding into the shadows was like being plunged into ice water, except the water felt like it was flowing through him, penetrating his whole body. His view of the world lost perspective and became more washed out. An unplaceable feeling, like the phantom weakness in one's knees when one walks over a grave, trembled through him. He held his breath and watched from the shadows. Jessie shook a little bit when she witnessed the maneuver. From her point of view, Alan was falling into his shadow like it was a pool of water. To her credit, she kept a steady expression in the face of the supernatural.

Once Alan and Blot were fully immersed in the shadows, the pendant lazily turned to face Frightful. Unlike with Blot, it was a much more wishy-washy sort of indication, but even an untrained eye could work out that it was trending in a single direction, and where the shadow creature could be found.

Blot released her grip. Alan surfaced like a life preserver slipping free from a sunken ship, bouncing into three dimensions again, now on the floor underneath the chair. The pendant oscillated back in their direction, with a brief hesitation as it swept past Chu-chu.

"All right," Blot said. "Still effective when we're in the shadow. Which means I *hope* the long-range effectiveness lasts as well." She flicked two of the thin sheets of paper, written in her own hand, out into the world again. "Jessie, this one's yours. You may not need it, because you still have your shadow, but it couldn't hurt. Just keep it on you."

"Can I leave it in my wallet?" Jessie said.

"Whatever. Probably. And this one, I have to put on Frightful."

Blot yanked it back into the shadows and approached the rikt. The silhouette creature seemed to stiffen as Blot got close.

"Steady, Frightful," Jessie said. "Be good. Treats if you're good."

The feathery edge of the shadow bristled. Blot flicked the little rectangle of paper and gingerly inched closer. Frightful produced a low, churring squawk. Blot froze in place, then suddenly whipped around the room, streaking across all four walls to appear behind Frightful in a dizzying blur.

Before Frightful could react, Blot slapped the slip onto the back of the rikt's neck.

In retrospect, it perhaps wasn't the wisest way to go about it. Frightful released something between a caw and a screech, a sound that managed to transcend language by being at once entirely animal in nature and yet a perfectly articulated "How dare you?" The bird launched from Jessie's shoulder and started chasing Blot around the room, bouncing from cabinet to "Live, Laugh, Love" frame to kitty-cat clock. Despite being ostensibly pursued by a predator, Blot giggled as she wove tight circles around the walls, staying just ahead. Not to be left out, Chu-chu zipped along after them, bouncing off Frightful and retreating to the shadow of a metal bowl fast enough to send it clanging to the ground.

"Frightful! Frightful, you come back here this instant. That's a *bad rikt*," Jessie scolded and held her arm up again. "Come!"

The larger of the rikts landed on the shadow of the chair, teetering it backward. Blot nudged it to keep it from tumbling over. The motion gave Jessie something to scowl at.

"*Now*, Missy," she said.

The rikt blinked her eye once, then hopped over to the offered arm to perch.

"Good. That's better. We play *nice* in this house," Jessie said, scooping out more kibble from her pocket. "Now, do we do the amulet again?"

"Yep? You ready, Alan?" Blot said.

"As I'll ever be."

She hugged him into the shadows once more. Jessie held up the amulet and gave it a spin. It ignored Blot, and this time ignored Frightful as well. The only unnatural motion to suggest it was anything but a standard piece of jewelry was when it slowed its rotation slightly each time it spun past Chu-chu.

Blot eased Alan and herself to be cast upon the chair, then allowed him to pop back into the world.

"That's a success!" Blot said. "I just have to make one for Chu-chu and we'll be as well-hidden as we're ever likely to get."

"Congratulations on learning magic!" Jessie said.

"Yeah. Shows what my teachers know. Back home they said I wasn't 'adequate' to 'waste resources' on trying to teach me." She crossed her arms. "I could have been a proper soldier if they'd given me the chance. I could've learned all sorts of magic. Rumor has it the most powerful Shade mystics had ways of temporarily blotting out the *sun*. That should have been my job. Blot is my *name*."

"Look at the bright side," Jessie said. "If you'd been a soldier, we probably wouldn't have joined forces. Things would have been much different. And if you ask me, much worse."

"Yeah," Blot muttered under her breath. "The *bright* side."

"Pardon?" Jessie said.

"The food's getting cold, and so's my coffee," Blot said. "Eat up. I'll get working on the spell for Chu-chu."

Blot drifted out of the kitchen and lurked in the living room. After a moment, she clucked her tongue and Chu-chu darted after her. Jessie picked up the gooey cheese sandwich and pulled it apart.

"Oooh... Look at that stretch..." She dunked it in the gravy and gave it a nibble. "So good... but I can feel my arteries hardening."

"She does like to make food that sticks to the ribs," Alan said.

He sipped the soup. It wasn't like any tomato soup he'd ever tasted. It was rich and intensely smoky, both from the bacon and from some sort of intentional char. The flavor was, to put it lightly, experimental. But not bad. The gravy was a little potent too. But the sandwich was divine.

"Blot!" Alan called over his shoulder. "My compliments to the chef!"

Blot made a noncommittal half sound in reply, though she failed to hide the dash of pride in her tone.

"Good for her. Learning new skills. Picking up new hobbies. You could learn a thing or two from her," Jessie said.

"I'm learning new skills. I'm doing that forensic photography elevated certification on Tuesday, remember?"

"I meant about the hobby."

"I have my photography," he said.

"That's your job. That's *two* of your jobs."

"My two jobs are photography of scandalous things and criminal things. My hobby is photography of beautiful things."

"I guess if you're going to be a one-trick pony, you picked a good trick."

Frightful blinked, then half lidded her eye. With a huff of a sigh, she stooped down and curled into Jessie's shadow.

"Oooh," Jessie said with a shiver. "It tickles when she does that. Makes me feel good that she's cuddling up like that more and more. Like she feels at home with me. A relief, too. If she felt like moving on, I'd be left without a way to see the stuff that's been going on. And a cuddle sure beats having her pinch my arm with those talons. Oh! Drinks!"

She stood and paced to the fridge. "Cider okay?" she asked over her shoulder.

"Fine by me," Alan said.

"We sure are lucky Frightful decided to pair up with me," Jessie said. "And that she's such a good little birdy."

"Something tells me it wasn't luck."

"What do you mean?"

"I get the feeling the rikts are a lot smarter than we give them credit for. And Gladys keeps a bunch of them around like the Shade-equivalent of a crazy cat lady."

"You think she told one to come find me?"

"I think maybe she's taught them to find the people that are worth finding."

"Nice to be considered worth finding, then," she said. "I notice Chu-chu doesn't pay you much mind."

"I'm either a perch or something that happens to be holding meat sometimes," Alan said.

"Why do you suppose that is?" Jessie said.

"Because he's *my* little rikt, that's why," Blot said, drifting through the room to start working on another coffee. "Plus, Alan doesn't have a shadow of his own. From Chu-chu's point of view, Alan basically doesn't exist. It's a *little* weird that he can perch on him. I think maybe Chu-chu is perching on the false shadow that the non-Shade-enhanced folks see. Which is surreal even for me."

Alan crunched at the wonderfully spicy cheese sandwich and balanced the flavors of the soup and gravy with sips of cider. As he ate, he watched Jessie shut her eyes and savor the meal. Behind her, Blot prepared a cup of coffee and happily cradled its shadow.

Another step had been taken to keep himself and his friends safe. Jessie was becoming a more adept keeper of the beast that just might prevent her from falling prey to evil Shades. No one had tried to kill them in weeks.

"Heh," Alan remarked.

"What's funny?"

"I don't have a knot of anxiety in my gut."

"Could be that things are actually looking up, huh?" Jessie said.

"They've certainly been worse," Blot said. "I could almost get used to this."

"... a nice dinner. We talked about hobbies. Got some work done," Alan said, completing the carefully edited account of the evening. In his telling, there were considerably fewer mildly obedient shadow birds and a few more jigsaw puzzles.

"Good, good!" the doctor said, scribbling something into her pad.

"She finished by underlining 'evasive' again," Blot said. "You need to get better at lying."

"I'd like to talk about your feelings of obligation. Your need to protect your family, your friends."

"I think—" Alan began.

"Tell her no. Tell her you're fine now."

"—I still struggle with them. The world feels so dangerous now—"

"No it doesn't. You're making good progress. Say that. Say you're making good progress."

"—I can't help but feel like there are things out there waiting to hurt them. I know it's silly—"

"We're trying to convince her we're *sane*, Alan. Quit actually telling the truth," Blot reprimanded.

"—but it feels very real to me," Alan said.

The doctor scribbled something again.

"And quit pausing suddenly like that. She's noticing," Blot said. "You've got to learn to listen and talk at the same time."

The doctor turned to a new page. "I'd like to talk about your coping mechanism. I think we should both be comfortable calling it that by now," she said.

"If she's talking about me..." Blot rumbled.

"Coping mechanism?" Alan said.

"You seem to have a schism in your thinking," she said. "It's not uncommon. We all have rival trains of thought vying for attention. But I've noticed you've taken to addressing yours on occasions."

"Not in *two whole sessions*," Blot countered. "You haven't slipped and said something to me since that first time."

"So what's up," Alan said. "Do you think I have multiple personality disorder? Schizophrenia or whatever?"

"That's not what schizophrenia is. These days we'd use the term 'dissociative personality disorder,' and no, I'm not suggesting you suffer from it. You don't exhibit distinct personalities. As I've said, this is what I'd call a coping mechanism. You've assigned certain invasive thoughts—what you likely consider the darker side of your personality—to a separate part of yourself. By separating those thoughts, you seek to create distance between yourself and the notions you wish didn't exist. Again, a perfectly common psychological mechanism. But most do not elevate it to the point that one speaks aloud to the keeper of those thoughts. And there is a pronounced verbal and physical tic when the subject turns to stresses in your life that I feel are a connected phenomenon."

"I now feel justified in stealing her legal pads," Blot said, stretching across the room to vanish through the crack of a locked cabinet.

"I don't know if I'm, um... ready to let go of that, Doc," Alan said.

"I know. And I'm not asking you to. Coping strategies exist for a reason. We need them. They're only a problem when they cause more stress than they relieve. If sticking a name tag on the chest of your darker thoughts helps you acknowledge and control them—"

"I wouldn't say I'm controlling them very well," Alan interjected, watching as three of the pens in the cup on her desk sank into their own shadows.

The doctor smiled. "Regardless. If embodying that part of yourself as something that can be called to task and reprimanded helps you sublimate feelings that you feel are unsuitable, then I don't want to take that tool away from you. Instead, I suggest a two-pronged approach. In the long term, I want you to learn to embrace that part of you. Accept that those thoughts are valid, acknowledge them as your own. Know that thinking those things, feeling those feelings, doesn't mean you'll act on them. And I think you'll find that over time you'll feel less compelled to foster the divide. And if they are as tightly linked with these feelings of obligation to protect your loved ones as I think, simply being with your friends, being with your family, and seeing that they are just as savvy and capable of their own protection as you are will help ease the tension as well. And in the short term, do you keep a journal?"

"No I don't," Alan said.

"I think you should start. If I may suggest a structure I believe will help you, try addressing each entry as though you were talking to the keeper of your darkness. Have you picked a name for him?" she asked.

"Her, actually," Alan said.

"Hey!" Blot said. "We're pretending I'm not *here*, remember? I'm not really the 'keeper of your darkness.' As though that's a bad thing."

"So you probably do have a name picked out, then," the doctor said. "Try it tonight. Open a file on your computer, or buy a dedicated pad and pen, and each evening, write out a message to her. Talk to her the way you'd talk to a friend. Someone who means well but who is causing you stress. Remember. She's a part of you. You can't hate her without hating yourself. And hating yourself will only deepen the scar. Accept that part of yourself, and I am quite sure you'll find it misbehaves less and less."

"Fat chance," Blot said.

"I think that's our time for today," the doctor said. "You're making good progress, Alan. Keep at it."

"Thanks, Doc. I'll try."

Alan got back into his car. Blot slid into the passenger seat and produced one of the pads and a pen.

"I'll give her this," Blot said. "She has good taste in pens. None of those stubborn blue ballpoints. A nice black rollerball."

"I really wish you wouldn't steal from her," Alan said, starting the engine.

"And I really wish you'd ditch her. She's going to keep on trying to put a mental bandage on me. And no matter how much she tries that nonsense, I'm not going away."

"It's complicated," Alan said.

"It isn't. The thing that's wrong with you is me, and I'm intractable," Blot said.

"You aren't the thing that's wrong with me," Alan said.

"Mmhmm," Blot said, scribbling on one of the stolen pads. "I need to find a legal-size clipboard. These pads are too floppy."

"I can just *buy* you a clipboard."

"Eh. I'm sure I'll find one lying around."

"That's called *stealing*, Blot," Alan rumbled.

"Only if I get caught."

"It's stealing even if you don't get caught. Stop changing the subject."

"Right, right. You were explaining how the human head doctor was somehow *not* going to label any evidence of my existence as a mental illness that needs to be corrected."

"I'm not saying she wouldn't say that. I'm saying it isn't true."

"Well if she's going to say it, then what's the point of going to her?"

"Because there are other things wrong with me."

"You're fine."

"You've seen my dreams. They're not the dreams of a man who is fine."

"They're the dreams of a man who is being either hunted by or recruited by arcane forces of at least two varieties, and arcane *organizations* of at least two varieties. While at the same time having to earn money to live." She flipped a page and doodled a bit. "Capitalism was a bad idea."

There was a time, not so long ago, that Alan had never heard of, nor dreamed of, things called Shades or Glints. Likewise the words "Dawn" and "Dusk" hadn't been the sort of things that required capital letters. But now he lived in a world where shadows had names, white-suited angels could compel him to act simply by speaking, and secret cabals aligned against each of them wanted a piece of Alan. It was a shame you seldom got a chance to enjoy your own ignorance until it was gone.

"We can agree about that much. But I think maybe it's a good idea to iron out some of the other wrinkles in my head so I can be at my best for when a random stranger's shadow starts hurling broken glass at me."

"Mmm..." Blot said, not willing to entertain the possibility that he was correct, but no longer interested in contradicting him.

The pair drove in silence for a few minutes.

"How are *you* holding up?" Alan said.

"Better than you. I'm learning magic. I'm learning to cook. A Shade could get used to a life like this. Why?"

"Because I care about your well-being."

"And?"

"And there doesn't need to be another reason."

"Yeah, but there *is* one," Blot said. "I can tell. You were setting up something."

Alan huffed. "You've been a little... testy lately."

"Was I ever *not* testy? It's part of my charm."

"More than the charming amount. Is something new bothering you?"

"Don't worry about it."

"See, this is something my mom does. You put me in a corner here. On one hand, if I want to be sure you're okay, I have to pry. And on the other, if I pry, it might make you less okay."

Blot held up the drawing she'd been working at. "Does this look like Chu-chu to you?"

"You're changing the subject."

"And what's that tell you about my opinion of the subject, Alan?" she said flatly.

"Fine. Just, you know. Speak up if you need me to do something."

"You want to do something nice for me? Get a better kitchen. We don't even have a broiler."

"It's not the sort of thing I can just *add*. We live in an apartment."

"Jessie has a broiler."

"Jessie had a better job when she got her apartment. I'm not going to be able to persuade my landlord to upgrade my oven."

"Just tell him that you're tired of producing inferior scalloped potatoes. That cauliflower au gratin I made last week was positively pale."

"I'm not sure it will be as persuasive as you think."

"Fine. ... How about a brûlée torch?"

"That I can do," he said, flipping the turn signal and plotting out the route to the home-goods store in his head.

"Great! Then stop and get some eggs and a bag of sugar, too. *Something* is getting caramelized tonight."

She reached her shadowy hand into his pocket and fetched a smooth, flat river stone. To a normal observer, the stone was entirely mundane. To Alan, the top bore a dark symbol that looked like a shadow that wasn't being cast by anything. Blot had smeared it there with her finger, and it had labeled the stone as Chu-chu's preferred perch. She gave the stone a shake.

"Chu-chu-chu," she trilled until the rikt uncoiled from it. "I drew you a picture!"

The single visible white eye blinked at the doodle. After a peck or two that convinced the rikt that the paper wasn't food, he squawked quietly and transferred to the shadow of the headrest to gaze through the tinted window.

"Pick up something raw and meat, too," she said. "Chu-chu needs his snacks."

"Between coffee and sausages, you two are getting to be kind of expensive."

"Either stop complaining about me stealing things or stop complaining about having to buy them," Blot said.

"Fair enough," Alan said.

One trip to the fancy grocery store later, they had a brown bag filled with all the fixings to make something that one would need a French accent to pronounce correctly. Alan pulled into the parking deck and started to breathe a sigh of relief as he noticed his neighbor Mrs. Levitt hadn't blocked his spot with her car today. The sigh caught in his throat when he spotted a figure standing squarely beneath the overhead light in front of the door to the apartment complex. The loitering man had small round glasses, a dark blue coat with silver buttons, a cane with a silver tip, and a long white beard. Alan wasn't sure of his name, but he was sure of one thing—the man was bad news.

"Tell me that isn't the old man from the Dawn," Blot rumbled.

"Mr. Fontaine," shouted the old man, his voice echoing through the parking structure.

"Hit him! Run him over!" Blot said.

"No. We're still in a truce with them... I think. And even if we weren't, I'm not going to just run someone down."

"Then let me do it. I know how to drive," she said, her shadowy hand reaching for the wheel. "I can do it at least well enough to run someone over."

"You touch this steering wheel and I'm taking the shades off the bedroom window," Alan snapped. "No killing without good reason."

"Fine... but I'll be keeping track of good reasons," Blot said.

Alan nearly scraped his car along Mrs. Levitt's minivan in his attempt to keep his eyes on the old man while he parked. He opened the door.

"Mr. Fontaine," the old man repeated, more quietly.

"I trust this isn't a business call," Alan said.

"What other reason would I have for contacting you? I'd like a word with you on a rather important matter that concerns all of us." He glanced at where Alan's shadow would have been if Blot hadn't slid aside to cast herself on the car beside him. "All three of us, in fact."

"The only thing that concerns *me* right now is *him*. I'm going to get the brûlée torch, just in case..." She slid through the car window.

"Forgive me if I don't invite you into my apartment," Alan said.

"Forgive *me* if I refuse to set *foot* in your apartment. This little chat needs to happen somewhere neutral. I have a place in mind—"

"Not a chance," said Alan and Blot at the same time.

"I'm not keen on you picking the spot," Alan continued. "Whatever you need to say, you say it right here in this parking garage."

"I liked you better when you were a little more naive, Fontaine," he said.

"I *bet* he did," Blot grumbled.

"Very well then," the old man said, after a moment of consideration. "Better to get it over with quickly than to argue. And this won't take long. The Dawn has been terribly busy of late, and we've had a *disproportionate* number of, shall we say, setbacks."

"My heart bleeds," Blot snarked.

"Setbacks?" Alan said.

"To be perfectly frank, if I had the numbers at my disposal, I would likely have put a few people on you, keeping an eye, because if I didn't know better, I'd suggest you'd decided this truce was chafing at you."

"I don't go back on my agreements, sir," Alan said.

"Yeah, we need to work on that," Blot said. "Going back on a few of your agreements would really help us out now and then."

"I'd love to take your word for it, but I can't afford to. There's too much at stake. As it happens, though, my suspicions have moved elsewhere. Your little *theft* had a great deal of information about us, but not enough to be making such precise strikes against us. This is deep knowledge. Closely held. That phone you stole wouldn't have been enough. There is a leak elsewhere."

Blot scoffed. "We could have gotten more information if we wanted it. He's underestimating us. All I needed was a cell phone and four little numbers last time and we learned the names and numbers of half their crew. Now I know how *computers* work."

"And then there's the matter of the Metro Ghoul. While we couldn't spare the people to watch *you* particularly closely, low-level threat that we imagined you to be, we *did* have members dedicated to keeping track of the Metro Ghoul whenever possible. You don't let a shade who's managed to become a serial killer lurk about without keeping tabs on him. He was a slippery one, but we observed at least one of your clashes with him. You're more formidable than we've given you credit for. If you wanted to be a thorn in our sides, you would have been a much *bloodier* one."

Blot made a sound of quiet satisfaction at their martial prowess being acknowledged.

"I'll be frank. We need help," he said.

"Kick him in the knee," Blot suggested.

"What kind of help?" Alan asked.

"A series of thefts has struck our local storehouses for Shade-specific weaponry. We are at this point *critically* underequipped. It is a small mercy—and a point of no small amount of suspicion—that the thefts have been conducted without violence. I'm not willing to call it good fortune that lives were spared. More like strategy. And more to the point, stealing our goods out from under our noses required intimate knowledge of our defenses, our schedules, our procedures... This is a deep, *deep* leak."

"And that's why you're coming to me. You need someone outside the Dawn to act on this. Someone whose actions couldn't be part of another leak."

"More or less."

"How about less," Blot suggested. "Don't do it. We don't need him, and even if he needs us, we don't care."

"I have my own problems," Alan said.

"Wait! Ask how he'll make it worth our while!" Blot said quickly.

"There's something in this for you, you realize," the man said.

Blot tipped her head and slid a bit farther behind Alan.

"I'm not looking for a bribe or a payment," Alan said.

"I'm not offering one. This is about what you're doing for *you*." He pointed at where Alan's shadow ought to be with the tip of his cane. "That *associate* of yours dies, you die, let's not forget. And someone out there has a heap of our equipment. Some of our most dangerous stuff. Things you haven't seen yet. Things you'd only ever see once, if you get my drift. With us? You have an understanding. A truce. With whoever's doing this? Who knows?"

"So he wants us to go face them directly? This guy doesn't know the first thing about manipulating someone through enlightened self-interest," Blot said.

"Facing someone armed with your gear is a reason *not* to do this," Alan said.

"I thought you might say that," he said.

The old man reached into his coat. Alan tensed. Blot snapped the brûlée torch out of the bag on the seat, ready to use it as a weapon. It was probably best that she'd not learned how to ignite it yet, because she'd forgotten the window was shut and simply clinked it off the glass. The motion and sound drew the old man's gaze, but he remained impressively steady.

"Your 'friend' is a little trigger-happy," he said.

"Yeah, well, there's a hole in my gut I had to heal up that says it's better to be trigger-happy than give this guy enough rope to hang me," Blot said.

The old man revealed what he'd reached for. It was a note, though the contents were illegible to Alan. The letters were arcane in nature. He handed it over.

"I suspect your friend can read that for you," the old man said.

Blot took it from Alan, holding it out mostly in a transparent desire to unsettle the member of the Dawn with overt usage of her mystical powers.

"One more major cache to clear up, then we take care of the traitorous liability. I want the"— Blot paused, glancing at Alan—"photographer dead. Make an example of him."

"Well?" the old man said.

"Where did you get this?" Alan said.

"We aren't entirely helpless. We have determined how some of the dead-dropped messages are delivered."

"Give me a minute," Alan said. He turned and spoke almost silently. "Could this be legit?"

"I think it almost certainly is," Blot said. "They might have learned how to read and write our language, but I don't think they'd have formed the word 'photographer' in that way. It's... it's an *old* combination of words. More of a... well, I'll tell you later. It's legit."

Alan turned back and handed over the slip of paper. "So they're after us," he said.

"Once they finish one more strike against our equipment reserves. It would behoove you to prevent that. And to get the gear back so when they decide to mop up the spilled milk that is your little partner, they'll at least not have the teeth of the Dawn to sink into it."

"So what *exactly* do you want us to do?"

"Find the leak and either point us to where our gear has been hidden or bring it back to us. And, while we're on the subject of what you can do for us, maybe you'd like to enlighten us how exactly the Shades have been hiding so flawlessly from us. Including *you*, of late."

Alan glanced aside at Blot.

"You're checking with that thing an awful lot," the old man said. "Who wears the pants in this relationship?"

Alan tightened his jaw. "I'm checking with *her* because she is as much a part of this as I am. And you're not getting on my good side with cracks like that."

"Play hardball. Ask him about Shards of Shadow before we give him a hint about how they're hiding," Blot said.

Alan took a deep breath. "I know the Dawn has Shards of Shadow. I don't know precisely what they *are*, besides powerful mystical artifacts. But the Dawn definitely has them. We learned that back at the prison."

"And?"

"How many? Where?" Alan said.

The old man laughed mirthlessly. "You know something? A few weeks ago I would have spat in your face before answering a question like that. As of three days ago, the question is yours to answer, not mine. The shards were the first things they took."

"How many?" Alan asked.

"Enough."

"You want my help, you answer me," Alan said.

"That's more like it," Blot said.

"Three," he said reluctantly.

"Fantastic," Blot said, eyes wide and practically sparkling. "This might be worth it after all. We get their gear, we get the shards, we *keep them*, we give a couple to Gladys in exchange for more training and to see if she can do her little project, and we keep one for ourselves. I say we do it."

Alan nodded in full agreement, if not with her motivations, at least with her conclusion. He turned to the old man. "We'll do it. And I can't say for certain how the Shades are hiding, but I can tell you it is by way of some of *your* magic."

"Our magic... so it's all part of the same leak, then," he said. "And you? I imagine you've probably found a different way to hide."

Alan silently glared at him.

"Fine. Keep your secrets. I don't have the time to waste arguing with you about it."

He reached into his coat again. This time Blot was able to restrain herself. He revealed a small, folded packet.

"The best intelligence we have about where and how the Shades have been operating. I can only hope the leak didn't include that info, or it won't do you much good." He handed it over. "We'll keep working at things on our side. We don't have a choice. But if you're thinking of double-crossing us, keep in mind just how much your Shade's people hate it right now. Stabbing us in the back is cutting off your own nose to spite your face. We'll be in touch."

The old man walked away, the silver tip of his cane clacking against the cement floor as he went. Alan watched him go, barely allowing himself to blink until the old man was out of sight.

"Well... so much for easing my anxiety," Alan muttered.

Chapter 2

It was too early, and Alan hadn't gotten much sleep. The business with the Dawn and the Shades had occupied his mind. It wasn't that it took that long to go through the notes they'd been handed. There was barely anything to them, the whole packet boiling down to the strong suspicion that Baltimore, Maryland, was the center of things right now. If not the center of their anti-Dawn operations, then the center of something else that was very important to the most-active Shades in the area. The rest of the night had been occupied by a potent combination of worry and research. The results of the night were twofold. First, there didn't seem to be a single thing in Baltimore that was of particular interest to the Shades; and second, Alan was *very, very* tired.

Sleep or no, it was one of his days off from being on call for his forensic photography job, so he was at the morning scrum at Cox Media, hoping for a photography assignment that didn't involve blood or broken glass for once.

"I can't believe Cox has got you back to standing out here waiting for handouts like a common nobody," Blot said from inside Alan's bag. "Your shots from the Metro Ghoul clash were all over TV *and* the newspapers *and* the internet. That must have made him a mint."

As the open floor plan of Cox Media wasn't conducive to Alan's attempts to keep things dim for Blot's sake, he'd made a habit of standing in the one spot that was gently shadowed by a column. It was enough to give Blot the ability to just barely slide herself into the darkness of his shoulder bag, where she had his phone so that she could continue doing research.

"Cox is a very 'what have you done for me lately?' kind of guy," Alan muttered quietly. "No meaty exclusives today, no private assignment meeting tomorrow. Any progress?"

"Not only can I not find any reason the Shades might want to collect in Baltimore, I can't find a reason why *anyone* would want to collect there. I'm really starting to doubt the Dawn did their homework right."

"There must be something halfway decent to pitch as an assignment from Cox."

"There are sports games... I see a carnival... a festival for crabs... or about crabs? Do you people worship crabs? Because they seem to be all anyone talks about in Maryland."

"I don't have an explanation. But I also don't think Cox would go for any of that."

"Look, does it matter? You could just take time off. We're not *that* hard up for money. We don't need this to be paid for by Cox."

"I'm Cox's best photographer. He needs the money I bring in. If we do it as an assignment, he's not losing work."

"Who cares about *him*? You know what your problem is? You're allergic to letting people down."

"That's not a bad thing."

"Oh, it's great for *other* people. And I guess I shouldn't complain, because I'm one of the other people. But I don't know if you've noticed, but you do that for everybody, and only two or three people do it back."

"I'm not doing it for what I get in return."

"I sure hope not, because—"

"All right! Listen up! Pickings are slim, so if you want a halfway decent assignment, you better be looking bright-eyed and bushy!" bellowed the perpetually dyspeptic Mr. Cox as he emerged from the office.

His face was a particularly vivid shade of hypertension red, and the typical stack of handwritten index cards was about a third the thickness it usually was. Half of the would-be photojournalists, upon seeing how few jobs there were, quietly slipped out the back rather than waste their time hoping for crumbs. Alan stepped forward with the others and braced himself for an unpleasant conversation once he reached the front of the line.

A few minutes later, the once-bustling room was reduced to Alan, Mr. Cox, and three college-age kids who clearly had different opinions about the appropriate gear for this level of photography.

"The job posting said *photographer*. Where's your camera?!" Cox barked.

"I usually just use my phone," muttered the girl in a cowed tone that suggested she wasn't expecting to get yelled at today.

"A phone. A *phone*! Phones are for ordering pizza and wasting time in the bathroom, not—" He pinched the bridge of his nose. "You know what? Here. Head down to South Street. Hit the tourist spots. If you get anything I can use, I'll pay for it. But if you're looking to do this, take it *seriously* next time."

He split the remains of the pile evenly between the two other girls and stomped back toward his office, rumbling like a thunderstorm that had just about run its course.

"Mr. Cox? Mr. Cox!" Alan called, trotting after him.

"You got the airport assignment, Fontaine. It's the best I have today," Cox said. "Take it and be happy."

"Right, right. But I was hoping I could do another photojournalism assignment."

Cox stopped and turned, a hungry gleam in his eye. "You going to give me another prison riot from the inside?" he said. "I could use another prison riot."

"I wasn't really thinking in that direction."

"You have a knack for tracking down spectacle. What've you got?" Cox said.

Alan cleared his throat. Blot took the hint.

"Still don't have anything better than the crab festival," she said.

"There's a festival in Baltimore that—"

Cox turned and raised his hand dismissively. "Pass."

"But it's a crab festival!" Alan said.

Cox turned. "Wait. Stop everything. A *crab* festival? In *Maryland*? This changes everything. Is *Old Bay* involved?" He dropped the false enthusiasm. "Stop wasting my time, Fontaine. Time is money and I'm short on both."

"I think you should rethink that," remarked a voice from the entryway.

Alan froze at the sound of the voice. Blot practically rattled with irritation. All turned to the doorway.

A pale androgynous person of indeterminate age paced toward them. They wore white overalls and carried a small pad, flipped open to a page that was held in place with their thumb. Alan knew this person, though to use both the words "knew" and "person" stretched the definition of each. They called themselves Angel.

"And who the hell are you?" Cox barked.

"Just an interested party," Angel said.

He pointed. "Get the hell out! This is a private business. We're not open to the public. What the hell am I paying the building security for if they're going to let some Edgar Winters–looking—"

"You were mistaken about the Maryland Crab Festival. You have a good feeling about it, and see it as an excellent opportunity to acquire a great deal of high-value footage and imagery," Angel said.

Cox squinted at Angel, then turned to Alan. "How much money are we talking?" Cox said.

"It's less than two hours away by car. You let me expense the gas and tolls there and back. Maybe a meal or two. And we'll do the standard rate for the materials I get, rather than the premium in my contract," Alan said.

"We can all agree that is an excellent offer," Angel said.

"Do it," Cox said. "I'll make a note of it. But this better be good. And give me that card back. I'm giving the airport to Marie-Anna." He marched to his office and slammed the door.

Angel tapped Alan on the shoulder. "We should go outside. We have matters to discuss."

"Kick them in the knee!" Blot shouted.

"You know, you never come along when things are going *well*," Alan said, marching out the door.

"I apologize, though in my defense, I suspect my mere appearance would at least, from Blot's point of view, disqualify a given moment as one that was going well."

Blot muttered to herself.

"We've been keeping an eye on things," Angel said.

"What else is new?" Alan said.

"A rather significant imbalance is new," Angel said. "The Shades have been heavily tipping the odds in their favor. And though it isn't entirely surprising, given certain circumstances which I am not at liberty to discuss, they have been doing so *without* bloodshed. We don't like that."

"You don't like that there's no slaughter going on?"

"We primarily don't like the imbalance, but the lack of slaughter is not without its concern as well. Naturally a massacre is not an ideal outcome, but it is one that has considerable precedent. Unprecedented tactics are, in our view, nonideal. They may produce unprecedented outcomes. And since most *desirable* outcomes have had precedent, it increases the chance of undesirable outcomes."

"You'd rather a ton of people die because you can predict how that'll end."

"Precisely!" Angel said with a smile. "I'm pleased I have articulated myself adequately. Now, I think it will come as no great surprise that we would like you to restore balance."

"How?"

"That is up to you. But when you are through, we need something more akin to a status quo than this burgeoning unstable equilibrium. If I'm frank, I would perceive the only reasonable solution to be the return of the stolen Dawn equipment to the Dawn. Simply destroying the equipment would be equivalent to doing nothing. Destroying huge swaths of the Shades?" Angel paused and consulted their book. "That, I suspect, would be acceptable as well."

"By the void, can that monster at least *pretend* not to want me and my kind dead?" Blot said.

"You're not giving me confidence that you have our best interests at heart," Alan said.

"What we have at heart is the desire to prevent chaos. That is what's best for us all. Because, after all, I am—"

"A human. Yes. You've said," Alan said. "Any chance you'll be offering us any assistance?"

"What do you suppose my advocacy, vis-à-vis the crab festival, was?" Angel said.

"I'm about to, potentially, go headfirst into a group of supernaturally powerful beings who have been scoring unanswered goals against the very organization that exists specifically to defeat them. I was hoping for something more tangible in the aid department."

"You don't want us taking direction action. That tends to be..."

"Nonideal?" Alan said.

"Again, I am pleased I have articulated my position so effectively. But if you *must* know, you *are* receiving more tangible aid, in that you are not being actively reprimanded for finding a way to hide from us."

"So it *is* working on them," Blot said triumphantly.

"I could simply order you to tell me how it's done," Angel said.

"Nope! Because *you* don't know how to do it, only *I* do and I'm a lousy teacher, so I wouldn't be able to tell you how to do it very easily," Blot said smugly.

"But we have decided that you can keep this semblance of privacy if it makes you feel more comfortable. You are a predictable person. We know where you live, we know where you work. We do not need to *mystically* detect you to watch you. And your stealth is incomplete regardless."

"How incomplete? Get them to tell me *how* incomplete," Blot urged.

"In what way is it incomplete?" Alan said.

"I am not at liberty to say. Good luck to you, Alan. I hope you can find a way to solve this problem that suits our requirements."

"That makes one of us..." Blot muttered.

Because Alan's "free time" came in vanishingly limited chunks, he didn't waste any of it debating what he should do and when. The moment he'd finished with Angel, he'd jumped in the car to head home, already running through the equipment he'd need.

"We should stop at the police station and steal some flash-bangs," Blot said from her place cast against the passenger seat. "We're running low on them."

"We shouldn't have *any* flash-bangs. When the police department finds out some of them are missing, we don't know what they'll do."

"Maybe not, but we know what they *won't* do, and that's assume their new forensic photographer's shadow is stealing them."

"They could just assume *I'm* stealing them."

"You don't have motive, means, or opportunity," Blot said. "I watch those police procedurals, same as you."

"... Still."

"That's the sound of you losing an argument."

"Does it take anything to keep that stealth magic working?"

"No. I just need to keep the slip of paper on me or on you. But I'll make backups. Oh, hey. There's a French fry in the seat. *Chu-chu!*"

The sun visor on the passenger side flipped down violently enough that it almost made Alan swerve the car into a guardrail.

"I really wish Chu-chu wasn't so good at hiding," he said as the avian shadow coiled down to perch on the emergency brake handle.

"It's his best trick. Treats, Chu-chu!" Blot said.

The rikt snapped up the French fry. Alan casually lowered the passenger-side window, which was presently in the shade. Chu-chu blinked once, then hacked the French fry out the window.

"And that's his second-best trick," Blot said.

"I don't know why you keep feeding him and why he keeps eating things that aren't meat when he doesn't *like* things that aren't meat."

"You never know. Maybe we'll find something else he likes."

Alan shivered. "We know something else he likes."

"Oh?" Blot paused, then shivered as well. "Oh..."

One of the only reasons the business with the Metro Ghoul had come to a definitive end was because rikts had a taste for weakened, hostless Shades. They'd seen the creature do its grim work once, and once was enough.

"A third thing, then," Blot said. "But back to planning. I've got your spare camera with me and those two big flashes. The batteries need charging. I also have one of those little GoPro cameras. I've been playing with it."

"To what end?"

"To a financial end. Never mind. I'll tell you if it works and I won't tell you if it doesn't. You just focus on making sure we don't run out of batteries."

"I'll grab extras when we get home. How about the flashlights?"

"I've got the big one and the small one."

"I'll grab the other two when we get in. And a bunch of D cells." He shook his head. "It's really starting to bother me how comfortable I'm getting with the idea of infiltrating a gang of supernatural enemies."

"Yeah, well, don't get used to it. We're walking a thin line. The only reason you're still breathing and I haven't been sent desperately searching for another host is because we're the rope in a tug-of-war. There's only three ways that ends. One side gets us, the other side gets us, or we snap. So the sooner we get ourselves set up to be safe and separate, the better. And unfortunately for me, you've got family and friends that need protecting, too. So the whole thing is a lot harder to handle."

"Speaking of... we need to call Jessie."

"Ooh. So Mr. Road Safety has to wait until a red light to pull out his phone and order coffees, but for *Jessie* it's 'we need to call her now,'" Blot said.

"You can be the one handling the phone when it's Jessie. She knows you exist."

"Yeah, yeah," Blot said, slipping the phone from his pocket and willing her hand out of the shadows to swipe out his password and tap Jessie's contact.

The speakerphone rang twice before she answered. "Hey, hey," she said. "Any good photo jobs this time?"

"Jessie, some stuff has happened," Blot said.

"What now?" she said seriously.

"The old man from the Dawn came and made a deal with us to help him go get their stolen gear, because if we don't, the people who stole it will slaughter them and then probably a lot of other people, and then the Glints came and told us they want us to do that too, so we're going to Baltimore."

Alan could practically feel Jessie's disapproving glare in the silence that followed.

"And I'm just learning about this *now*?" she said.

"You were asleep. You have to work the night shift tonight," Alan said.

"I don't like the idea of you doing this alone, Alan," Jessie said.

"He never does anything alone," Blot said. "He's got me and Chu-chu."

"You know what I mean. What are we looking at?"

"Don't know for sure," Alan said. "We only have the Dawn's information to go on, and it's pretty thin. Basically, a *lot* of Shades, and ones that are sneaky enough to steal from the Dawn."

"Steal from them? Not kill them?" Jessie said.

"So far," he said.

"That's good news, isn't it? Maybe they're nonviolent. Just trying to force peace through disarmament or something."

"We work pretty hard to weed out the nonviolent Shades before we send them over," Blot said. "*I'm* not even nonviolent so much as I was barely capable of violence when I started, and then *Alan* did me the disservice of turning out to be a decent guy. I don't think there'd be enough Shades willing or able to separate from the rest of us to form a group big and powerful enough to do something like this. Even Gladys and the so-called Dusk seem like the best they can do is keep their heads down."

"Then why keep it peaceful so far?"

"Maybe they're waiting until they know they can take out the entire Dawn at once? Maybe they're just hoping they can avoid retaliation if they don't kill anyone? I don't know. I was mostly trained in observation and manipulation. Combat and tactics were for better Shades."

"I don't like it, Alan. Are you going to be able to handle this?"

"This is the first time I know I'm getting into something. I don't know exactly what it is, but it's at least not getting the jump on me. That's new. And I survived all the times the problem *was* getting the jump on me. I wouldn't say I'm cocky, but I'm... no, I guess I wouldn't say I'm confident either. I'm less certain of my certain doom than usual."

"Baby steps," Jessie said. "I wish I could help you, but I feel like I'd be more of a liability than an asset, since at any moment, Frightful could just wander off and I'd be fighting blind."

"I'll keep him alive," Blot said. "Do you know how hard it would be to find another host who would buy me Kona Hawaiian whole bean coffee without me asking?"

"Listen, Jessie. I didn't want to worry you, but I also didn't want to—"

"No, no. You did the right thing. I'm the only other human you don't have to keep secrets from. I can't say I'll sleep better at night knowing what you're going through, but at least I know I don't have to worry about you running off to do this sort of thing without letting me know. Just promise me you'll reach out for help if you need it. Don't be a hero."

"That's what I've been telling him from the beginning," Blot said.

"I have neither pride nor bravado when it comes to butting heads with a conspiracy of Shades," Alan said. "If there's help, I'll ask for it."

"Good. Call as often as you can. If I'm asleep. If I'm on duty. I don't care. I need to know."

"Will do. And do me a favor."

"Anything."

"Keep an eye on Mom and Dad for me? If I was a murderous mastermind who wanted Alan Fontaine to suffer, waiting until he was out of town and then attacking his parents—"

"Understood," Jessie said.

"All right. Thanks. Talk to you soon," Alan said.

"Good luck, be safe."

Blot ended the call and slipped the phone back in Alan's pocket. After a few seconds of silence, Alan glanced in her direction and found her staring at him.

"What?" he said.

"Nothing. You just get a lot more relaxed after talking to her. Even if she yells at you."

"She's my friend. That's sort of the reason you *have* friends. To be each other's shelter in the storm."

"I'm your friend."

"Of course you are."

"So what do you need her for?"

"Don't start again with this," Alan grumbled.

"I'm not telling you to ditch her. But what's different about you calling her and her not being able to help at all yet somehow making you feel better, meanwhile *I'm* here literally watching your back and you stay a nervous wreck."

"I don't know... I... I guess it's because I know her from before, um..."

"Before *me*?" Blot said.

"Before I got involved in this insanity. She's like a connection to a time when I had much less reason to believe I'd wake up dead on any given day."

Blot twiddled her fingers to give Chu-chu something to chase. "Must be nice..." she said.

"Having a friend?" Alan said.

"Yeah. You've got me and her. All I've got is you."

"You've got her, too. She's your friend."

"Sure she is..." Blot muttered. "Somehow I don't see the two of us having any conversations without you at the center."

"That's more a logistical thing than a social thing."

"'Not friends for a good reason' is still not friends. But the joke's on you. I was lying about having no other friends. I've got Chu-chu." The rikt pecked at her finger, but she yanked it clear. "And at least *he's* not psychologically complicated."

"Now *that* must be nice," Alan said.

Chapter 3

Jessie paced along the streets of Philadelphia. Officially, police didn't really do the whole "walking a beat" thing. That's what patrol cars were for. But there wasn't an explicit rule *against* it, so she did it as often as she could. It was worth it.

"Evening, Mr. Green! How's Jason doing in college?" Jessie called across the street.

"Ugh. That kid is wasting my money. He should have gotten a job with the city and skipped college altogether," the older man grumpily called back.

"Give him time. College is about more than education, you know," she said merrily.

She had only recently been provided with clearance to leave desk duty, and under other circumstances, she would have been reveling in this moment. There were lots of reasons she'd become a cop. Some of them, it turned out, were based on a rather rosier picture of the role and capacities of a police officer than had turned out to be realistic. But she'd always prided herself on doing the job as she believed it was meant to be done. She followed the rules set forth by her superiors, but she followed them in the way that a "good cop" would follow them. And part of that, she felt, was being a part of the community she was policing. It was possible to begin to feel separate from one's city when the streets you patrolled during work hours were different from the ones you lived and played in when you were off the clock. Jessie didn't go in for the "thin blue line separating order from chaos" interpretation of her job. In her view, police shouldn't be separating anything from anything. She was a *part* of the community that was helping it stay safe. And the best way to do that was to actually be visible in the neighborhood in capacities beyond enforcing the law.

"Julie! I haven't seen you since you cut your hair! Looks great!" Jessie called to another friendly face, earning a cheerful thanks in reply.

Alas, two very substantial changes to her life were preventing her from fully indulging her mind in this cherished part of her profession. The first was that there existed forces with very real influence over the health and safety of her friends and neighbors that, until recently, she'd not known existed. She'd had to visit Alan's parents before she started her shift not because it was the neighborly thing to do, but because there was the nonzero chance that they'd been targeted by foes they couldn't even conceive of. That Alan was in a car and driving to unfamiliar territory to clash with these foes was simmering in the back of her mind, making her feel a constant low-grade anxiety. The second change to her life was the mechanism by which she'd developed the ability to *see* this previously unseen threat.

"You doing okay, Frightful?" she whispered, glancing at her shadow.

It was dark enough that the rikt could remain perched upon the shoulder of her shadow rather than having to nestle into the shadow itself as tended to happen in full sunlight. She'd had difficulty grappling with the exact nature of the rikt. Intellectually she was aware that it was a being that existed *only* as a shadow—at least in *this* world. But wrapping her head around that proved more abstract than she was willing to think. So she'd come to imagine that it was a real bird, physically present but invisible, that cast a shadow she could see. Why "an invisible bird is sitting on my shoulder" was easier for her to grasp than "a shadow bird is sitting on my shadow" was a mental quirk she probably would have enjoyed discussing with her therapist if she were able to. For now, she just accepted that it was the bandage she needed to slap onto the situation to make it feel less maddening.

She smiled at Miss Turner, whose dog just had puppies. She held the door for Johnny, who was trying to carry a full week's worth of groceries up the steps in one go, as usual. Then, at the edge of her hearing, Frightful made a threatening squawk. It drew her attention to an unfamiliar man, her eyes flicking to his shadow.

For half an instant, she saw a pair of white eyes staring at her from the shadow. They shut tight, but not quickly enough to convince Jessie that she was seeing a trick of the light. She kept her expression sunny and unchanged, hoping to avoid tipping the Shade off that it had been spotted. A bolt of anxiety seared at her gut, and her mind started quickly circling the wagons to work through the possibilities.

Frightful was visible on her shoulder for those with Shades, so there was no possibility for Jessie to pretend she was *entirely* normal. But Blot hadn't known that having a rikt perching on her would give her the ability to see the Shades, so it was just possible that other Shades didn't know either. But why would the Shade shut its eyes and hide? Perhaps it was hiding from the rikt? Frightful certainly had a low-grade hostility for any Shades she noticed. Even Blot was at best *tolerated*. But according to their telling of the events around the Metro Ghoul, Alan and Blot didn't know nearly how dangerous the rikts were to Shades before they saw them do their dirty work. She decided to lean on the potential that the Shade was simply being extremely cautious.

Then there was the matter that the Shades were *supposed* to be gathering down in Baltimore. That was the premise of Alan's trip there, anyway. But she supposed there was no reason to believe *all* of them would have collected there. It was probably a *lot* of them, though, because she'd seen very few Shades "in the flesh," for lack of a better phrase, besides Blot. In fact, Jessie had seen more of them in images and video than in real life. Watch the news often enough and a pair of spooky white eyes inevitably peered out of the shadows of people attending the high-class, high-influence gatherings that a power-hungry creature focused on world domination would want to attend.

The Shade-bearing person turned a corner. Jessie followed, doing her best to avoid seeming as though she was in pursuit. Now her mind took a new direction. One that had become a larger and larger part of her thought process the longer she was a cop. *Why* was she following this person? She had seen a Shade, yes. And she was told—and had significant evidence to support—that Shades were dangerous. But there was terrible risk in assuming that *all* Shades were bad just become some of them—or even *most* of them—might be. Blot wasn't bad. Blot was *so* not bad that countless lives had been *saved* because of her. Instinct, training, empathy, and common sense were all tugging and pulling at her mind as she rounded another corner and saw the Shade-bearing human step into a nondescript building.

It was a relief when he was gone from view. It allowed her to pull her mind away from assessing the human-Shade pairing and wondering if and how she could justify even placing them under suspicion, let alone under arrest. Now she could assess the building, which was a much less troublesome assessment. Even without knowing what to look for, she would have known there was something odd about this building. It was late, but not the dead of night. Most of the buildings around had lights shining around the edges of drawn shades or fancy curtains. Not here. Without exception, every window in the building was dark. The way the darkness was achieved varied from window to window. Standard, heavy drapes, probably blackout curtains, covered some of the windows. A few had newspaper, aluminum foil, or kraft paper stuck to the window.

If she didn't know better, she'd suspect it was condemned. Plenty of buildings marked for renovation or destruction seemed to have that sort of haphazard "don't look inside" sort of treatment. But nothing *else* about the building looked like it was on its last legs. The place was well cared for, and it was clearly in frequent use.

"What do you think, Frightful?" Jessie mused quietly. "Do we look into things?"

The rikt churred lightly and coiled into her shadow.

"I think we have to. But I'm not knocking on any doors unless I have good reason. First, we ask questions."

It had been a short drive from Philadelphia to Baltimore. Alan's journeys in his youth had mostly taken him north, either in the direction of New York City, where most photographers on the East Coast tended to congregate, or to Upstate New York, where the family land had been... and he supposed it still was, since the sale of the land still hadn't been finalized. So in his head Maryland had been the kind of place you'd take a road trip to, and not somewhere you could reasonably run to for lunch and be back by dinner. But arriving was only the first step. He *also* had to find where the other Shades were hiding.

When they'd arrived, the sun was still up, which would have made searching on foot unpleasant for Blot and Chu-chu, to say nothing of how much more ground they could cover in the car. But five hours of sweeping neighborhoods hadn't turned up anything suspicious. The best they could manage was a vague notion from Blot that something might feel a bit different about the section of town currently much harder to search thanks to the crab-focused street festival that was ostensibly their reason for coming here. Now, the sun was down and most of the street festivities had calmed to a simmer, so he could finally step out of the car and start searching on foot without being in the middle of a crowd of shellfish addicts.

"Anything?" he said, scanning the street ahead.

"Not since the last time you asked. I'll let you know if I find anything," Blot said.

"It's just that I kind of figured you'd be able to sense them," Alan said.

"The Glints sent us down here to do their dirty work, and all they do is watch people. Did you think we'd pop down here and have it be a walk in the park?"

"I guess not. Maybe I can ask around," Alan said.

"What are you going to ask?"

"I don't know. I'll try to be tactful. See if I can learn something."

"I guess it's better than nothing. Pick someplace dark so I can focus. While you're working the locals, I'll see if I can get my magical skills working."

Alan paced down the street. It probably shouldn't have come as a surprise that the part of town that Blot had guessed might have some Shades in it was in a part of town that Alan would have called shady even before he'd met her. He didn't know if the placement of the festival here was intended to revitalize the area, but it was clear to him the neighborhood could certainly *use* it. More than half of the streetlights were broken. It was the part of a major city where you could feel the skin on your back twitch every time you turned away from an alley or doorway. Something deep inside him was absolutely certain a cartoon robber with a mask and a striped shirt was going to pop out and tell him to "stick 'em up."

In his search for someplace that fit the criteria of "is dark, has people, and might not get him stabbed," he decided to focus on the first two and slip into a smoky bar. The buzz of a neon sign for a beer company that had been out of business for a decade buzzed louder than the jukebox. It, a handful of other neon signs, and a single hanging light over the pool table were the only lights in the place. The bartender was a heavily tattooed older woman who had a glare that probably took the place of a bouncer in this place, because the instant she turned to him, Alan felt like apologizing and slipping out again. It was almost certainly why despite there being plenty of festival stragglers about, this place seemed only to have locals and regulars.

He steeled himself, picked a bar stool that still had some of its original vinyl, and nodded in her direction.

"You want something?" the woman said, in a voice that was two decades older than the rest of her.

"Uh... Miller Light."

She took her time heading to the appropriate tap. Chu-chu, having apparently decided he'd been behaving himself for far too long, darted out of Alan's pocket. The sprite form of the rikt bounded from shadow to shadow, rocking assorted forgotten plaques and fluttering promotional posters. The motion didn't draw the attention of so much as a single patron. Most were visibly on the far side of the slide toward drunkenness. It would take a bucket of cold water to get half of these people to even look up from their drinks.

Chu-chu found his way to a bowl of peanuts that Alan wouldn't have eaten from if his life depended upon it. A single peck snatched up a nut. He braced himself for a hack to send the nut launching at someone surly, but Chu-chu apparently was able to stomach the snack, though not enough to go back for more.

"Your beer," she said.

He fished out the cash and a reasonable tip and tossed them on the bar. "So... uh... anything... *suspicious* been going on around here?" Alan said.

"Smooth," Blot snarked.

"You a cop?" she asked.

"No."

"You look like a cop."

"I'm a photographer."

"Finish your beer and run along, photographer."

"Right. Okay."

"Good news, Mr. Investigator. I'm getting something," Blot said. "It's weak. I need a few minutes to really get a sense for it."

One half-flat beer later, Alan was back on the street. Blot stretched herself out on the street before him, making use of the darkness afforded by the lackluster public lighting.

"I'm sure of it now... This way. Take it slow. They're close, and probably watching," Blot said.

Alan didn't bother sticking to the shadows the way he would if he was trying to sneak up on a human. He just walked slowly and carefully forward, eyes roughly in the direction Blot was casting herself.

"They're using the spell. A version of the stealth spell we learned about from the ghoul hunt. So the trick is tracking the spell and not the Shade. But it's not easy. It's like... a steady, half-silent tone. One of those beeps you can never quite place."

He continued forward, following her like the needle of a compass.

"We're close... It's stronger now," Blot said. "I can feel a few. Get a flashlight ready, just in case."

He nodded and reached a hand into his pocket, wrapping it around the cold aluminum body of a high-quality LED flashlight.

"Wait a minute..." Blot said, suspicion in her voice.

She suddenly darted forward, stretching herself almost to her limit to reach the base of one of the lampposts with the broken light. Alan dashed after her.

"By the void," she muttered as he arrived.

She cast her arm up along the pole and pointed. There, like someone had dipped their finger in shadow itself and smeared out a series of shapes, were some Shade runes.

"What is it?" he asked.

"It's the stealth spell. They inscribed it on a lamppost."

"Is that... a part of it? Are they mapping out an area it covers?"

"No. They're trying to hide the lamppost," Blot said. "It's a decoy. They know we can track the spell, so they're putting it up all over the place. There's another one over there. I can see it. We're definitely in the right neighborhood, because these didn't just *show up* here. But it's not going to be as easy as just tracking the spells."

"So what do we do now?"

She tapped her head. "I was hoping you'd have some ideas. This was sort of my plan, to track these spells."

"Can we wipe the spell away somehow? Clear it? That way we can narrow down the decoys and eventually find some real Shades."

"We can, but it'd probably take me longer to do it than it would for them to make a new one. We'd be fighting the ocean with a broom."

He tapped his fingers on his leg. "What if they're moving?"

She rubbed her hands together. "Yeah... yeah, I guess that's one way to tell them apart. But it was hard enough to find this thing while it was standing still. I'm *really* going to have to focus if we're going to detect something like that. And if I was a Shade doing business in this town, particularly one who had reason to believe someone had shown up and was looking for me, I'd wait until *much* later. After the moon had set. Something that would increase the chances that at any given moment a good pitch-black shadow was nearby to give me a chance to rise up and do some damage. So I wouldn't expect much motion until then."

"I guess I'll be finding somewhere to settle down and wait," Alan said.

"Preferably somewhere that sells coffee," Blot suggested.

Jessie finished the most recent circuit of her patrol back at the station and popped open her department-issued laptop on the desk she'd been so eager to get away from. She knew a few people would probably have just shown up at the apartment building and asked to look around if they'd had suspicions about what might be going on inside, but she tried not to stretch policies just because she had a hunch. Fortunately, the department's database was fairly up to date, even for the petty stuff. She punched in the address to see what sort of things had been going on in the area. The building itself was pretty clean. There had been a recent uptick in noise complaints. In the last two weeks, the number of traffic violations had quadrupled, but that just meant it was up from two to eight. A single party with no off-street parking could account for that. None of the telltale signs that a building had become a haven for criminals.

She broadened her search, but zooming any further out flooded the results with reports relating to the ATM heists that had been giving the department a black eye for months. Starting right around when Alan said the Shades had first shown up, there had been a massive rash of ATM robberies. Most of them happened over the same two-week period. Then came a lull. But in recent weeks, the number of thefts had risen to an unacceptable level and stayed there. Thieves—or maybe employees, if you listened to the current investigators—were skimming fifty to seventy-five percent of the cash in ATMs with almost clockwork regularity despite steadily increasing security precautions. Better surveillance. More security personnel. An expanded program of recording the serial numbers of every bill in every machine in Philadelphia. None of it had made a difference.

Jessie started clicking to hide the unwanted ATM theft alerts. She was absolutely certain the Shades were responsible for those, too, considering Alan had told the story of a Shade-bearer named Lenny who lauded the ease of getting cash as one of the things that made being the host of a Shade tolerable. But right now she had more important investigating to do. She stopped hiding the ATM theft notifications, though, when she realized something. They hadn't shown up until *after* she'd expanded the search. There were plenty of ATMs nearby the apartment building, but none of them had reported any thefts in a month. The immediate neighborhood around the building was one of the only multiblock chunks within Philadelphia's city limits that hadn't had a single ATM cleaned out during the crime wave.

She narrowed her eyes and flipped through the department's phone directory. She dialed the number for the power company.

"Hello, this is Officer Jessie Hearst at the Philadelphia PD. To whom am I speaking? ... Sarah, great. I have an address I'd like to run by you, to see if you've noticed any irregularities..."

Twenty minutes and six phone calls later, she hadn't learned very much, but there were some oddities. With regard to violations, there were very few. All traffic violations were paid in full at the earliest opportunity. Utilities were paid up. But according to a few direct conversations with payment processors, several of their bills were paid in cash, which was enough of a rarity that they had to use special procedures to facilitate it. It wasn't *much* of a stretch to draw a connection between a rash of cash thefts and an apartment building paying its bills in cash, but it was still a stretch. And it just so happened that the special procedures involved in processing a payment in cash included running the serial numbers against known cash thefts, and the bills were all clean.

"It could just be a coincidence. That could have just been a Shade and its host trying to live their lives, and the rest is me chasing smoke..." Jessie muttered, curling her fingers in midair and grinning at Frightful as the rikt rubbed against them and churred. "Or the clean bills could be the result of money laundering and this whole operation is more sophisticated than I thought."

She let the facts and theories bob about in her head for a few more moments, then shrugged. "When in doubt, appeal to those with greater experience," she said.

She stood and trotted downstairs. A police station was one of a handful of places where there was sure to be people working at all hours. Like the hospitals, hotels, and other all-night establishments that shared that status, employees tended to clump around sources of caffeine. In the station, the "good" coffee machine was on the first floor. She found three old-timers sitting in the abused folding chairs in the improvised break room, nursing coffees and giving each other the thousand-yard stare of someone who wasn't so much meeting with an associate as existing in proximity to another human being. As far as each of them was concerned, the others could have been a pile of dirty laundry and it wouldn't have altered their interaction.

"Hey fellas!" Jessie said, instinctively heading to the coffee machine to swap the filters and refill the grounds. "How are things?"

Two of them turned and squinted at her like she was shining a flashlight in their faces, unaccustomed to any degree of sunniness in the attitudes of people working this late.

"Officer Hearst," rumbled the oldest of them. It felt less like an acknowledgment than just an old man proving he remembered her name.

"Same ol', same ol'," said a younger man.

Notably, none of them asked how things were going with her, but that didn't matter, because she'd been planning to tell them regardless.

"So I've been looking at this apartment building on the south side of town, and there's something off about it."

"There's something off about the whole south side of town," croaked the older man.

"North side's a little off, too," the younger man said.

"I live on the north side," said the old timer.

"Like I said, a little off," jabbed the younger.

"All the windows are blocked off," Jessie said, hoping a little forward momentum would short-circuit the inevitable devolution into jabs about each other's neighborhoods. "A whole apartment building. I could see one or two, but the whole building?"

"It's undesirables cramming too many people in there," said the old man.

She suppressed the urge to roll her eyes. "I don't know if there's any evidence to support that."

"Have they been bothering other people?" he asked.

"There's been some noise complaints, but no more so than—"

"It's their loud music. Have they been blocking up the streets?"

She paused. "There's more parking tickets than usual for—"

"Illegals," he asserted, finally letting the veneer of abstraction fall away. "They come here, they stuff three families into one apartment, and they think if they just keep the curtains shut, we won't know any better. They think we're as dumb as—"

"Tell you what!" Jessie said, preempting further elder-griping. "I'm going to go grab a fresh bag of coffee grounds. This one's just about tapped. Thanks for the insight, fellas!"

She paced out of the room, the casual intolerance having subsided to a low rumble behind her. That particular officer was one of the elder statesmen of the office, and she liked to believe his particular brand of old-fashioned bias would be leaving the station when he retired in eight months. It was one of many soothing things she liked to believe despite strong supporting evidence to the contrary. But stripping away the *reasons* for his assessment, the assessment itself did hold water. Parking snarls and sound complaints *could* tell the tale of an apartment building groaning under the weight of too many occupants. And the Shades had demonstrated a tendency to congregate. Combine that with the fact that each individual who had a Shade technically counted as two, and there was the weak implication that the building might just be a headquarters for Shades.

It didn't move the needle on giving her just cause to directly investigate, but it reinforced her decision to keep a closer eye on it. If there was a gathering of Shades in town that had slipped past their observation, it was something that Alan should probably know about. And if they had a link to the chain of thefts from ATMs, it was something that she was duty bound to stop regardless of their supernatural nature. Laws were laws.

She was going to have to find a good corner store near the apartment building, because she was going to be spending a *lot* of time hanging around the neighborhood.

Chapter 4

Alan held his thermal mug like a life preserver as he paced after the dark figure of Blot extended before him. His early start at Cox Media and the long night of searching meant that he was now inching past the twenty-hour mark in terms of wakefulness. He rarely slept a full night, and on those rare occasions that he did, there tended to be a lucid moment or two where he was touching bases with Blot, who didn't sleep at all. It meant that he was operating at a very low capacity, and the coffee was the only thing keeping him reasonably sentient.

"Anything..." he muttered.

"Alan, I swear to darkness if you say 'anything' again, I'm going to lead you into oncoming traffic. Don't you think if I found something, I would have told you I'd found something? This isn't any fun for me either, you know."

"Sorry, sorry," he said, the outburst serving the purpose of a bracing splash to his brain.

"No," Blot grumbled. "It's fine. I just thought... I just thought I'd be better at this by now. Turns out writing down spells and changing spells that already work is a lot different from the mystic arts in general. I must have found fifty of those decoy stealth spells, so I'm getting good at finding those, but the ones that are shifting around? The best I can say is they're all, roughly, that way."

She pointed ahead to a cluster of streets they'd circled at least twice since they'd arrived. "I don't feel any motion outside of that area, and I do feel motion inside of it."

"How much motion?"

"A lot," she said. "Enough that I'm a little angry I can't narrow it down further. It's like I kicked a beehive, and I can hear that they're *angry*, but I can't see where they're swarming."

"Narrowing it down to one neighborhood is better than nothing." He tipped his cup back and found, to his horror, that it was empty. "Maybe it's time that I tagged in. We've got two brains working on this, even if it feels a little like one point three minds. Let's think about this from the point of view of our targets. Set aside the magic. It's past midnight. I'm a human with a Shade who probably has been pushing me a lot harder than you've been pushing me. Where am I going to end up?"

He pulled out his phone and swiped the words "all-night diner" into the search with his thumb. Only three of them fell within the indicated neighborhood. The nearest was around the next corner.

"We'll go in for a refill," Alan said. "And we'll keep our eyes open the entire time."

He trudged down the street toward a diner that, in accordance with an unwritten law, had a name that leaned far too heavily on a labored pun about clocks. Unlike the bar, the place was packed, with only a single place to sit on the unfavored bathroom side of the snack counter. It was also rather well lit, much to Blot's chagrin.

"I'll be with y'all in a minute!" called the frustratingly energetic young waiter running things for the evening.

Alan nodded and plopped down onto the uncomfortable stool.

"The coffee smells like death, Alan," Blot said, gazing up at him from where the overhead light cast her on the counter. "Gotta admire a place that goes for potency over quality."

"Yeah, I'm not sure that's by design," Alan said quietly.

He flipped up the laminated place mat that doubled as a menu and ordered something relatively innocuous. The waiter nodded through it, filled up a coffee without being asked, and vanished to serve other customers. Alan poured half of the coffee into his thermos to sip from, then strategically placed the mug so he could lean over it to cast Blot into a position where she could sip.

"Holy heck," Alan said, shuddering at the intensity of the coffee.

"This stuff is to coffee as syrup is to tree sap. They boiled away all the weakness," Blot said.

"For someone who has become a legit connoisseur of coffee, I don't know how you can stomach this stuff. I wouldn't be doing it if I didn't need it to stave off unconsciousness."

"Coffee can be good in different ways, Alan."

A plate of food was set before him with impressive efficiency. He felt the odd tingle of claws working their way up his side that signaled Chu-chu emerging from the stone in his pocket and clawing his way against the current of light. While Blot didn't sleep, and Alan couldn't be sure Chu-chu did either, the rikt certainly had a catlike tendency to curl up somewhere cozy and stay there for hours at a time.

"My big strong boy," Blot said, admiring the creature. "You're almost as able to fight the light as I am!"

Chu-chu heaved himself across the surface of the counter and struck the shadow of the napkin dispenser hard enough to make it wobble in place. Alan steadied it, then turned and held his hand out so that Blot's hand would match, providing a shaded route to the edge of the plate where the piece of sausage Alan had earmarked for the rikt was waiting.

"Getting anything now?" Alan said quietly.

"We're very close. There's a lot of motion. Faster than the other motion, which I think means it is closer," Blot said. "Can't focus on any of it specifically. We're definitely in the right neighborhood. I can feel it. Someone is close."

"All right. What can we do to narrow it down further? Is there something—"

"There!" she hissed.

Alan snapped his head toward the doorway, a motion that, in retrospect, may have been a trifle obvious. The moment he spotted the pair of men stepping into the diner, they froze in place, eyes fixed on Blot, who was in turn making eye contact with a Shade cast upon the floor.

The pair of men silently backed away.

"After them!" Blot urged.

Alan stood, nearly knocking over the stool. Chu-chu, sensing a chase was afoot, dolphin-dived across the shadows of the plates, jostling each of them, and vanished out the door. The rikt's figure hadn't even bothered to shift to its sprite form. It seemed downright agitated by the presence of the other Shades and could be heard outside, squawking something that probably would have been savage and threatening if rendered in a human tongue. Alan took one step toward the door when the waiter, moving with the speed and precision of a ninja, appeared in front of him.

"I *know* y'all aren't trying to leave without paying for your meal," he said, perfectly balancing the threat of reprisal with the benefit of the doubt.

"I—Sorry, I—There's something I—" Alan stammered.

A fresh sequence of jostling plates and glasses signaled the return of Chu-chu. The rikt was moving at a speed that could only be inspired by fear and struck the stone in Alan's pocket hard enough for the side of his jacket to whip around and strike him in the back.

"Someone let a squirrel in here or somethin'?" the waiter said, trying to figure out what had managed to tip over three different coffee cups.

"Forget it," Blot said. "They're moving too fast. I think they got pulled into the shadows. But there's a whole stir a little way further along. We're close enough that we're going to need a plan if we're going to get any deeper, especially now that we've been spotted."

"I, uh... thought I heard my car alarm. Sorry about that," Alan said, taking a seat.

"Lean over. I want to check on Chu-chu," Blot said.

Alan angled himself awkwardly so that Blot could be cast roughly in the right place to slip her head into his pocket. Something was definitely up with the rikt. He could feel it trembling in his pocket. After the waiter had finished mopping up spilled coffee and had topped off the mugs that had been emptied, he huffed a sigh of relief and leaned on the counter in front of Alan.

"So you're new. Don't get a lot of new faces in this part of town at this time of day," he said.

"Yeah. Just visiting."

"In for the festival?" he said.

"Right. Yeah," Alan said. "You say you don't get a lot of new faces in here. Did you happen to know those two guys who changed their mind about coming in here a minute ago?"

"Uh...yeah. They've been around. They're pretty new, I guess. First showed up a couple weeks ago. But they're in here so often they got upgraded to regulars pretty quick."

"A couple of weeks," Alan said. "Any idea what they do?"

"They eat runny eggs and they're pretty lousy with their tips. Why all the curiosity?"

"I'm sort of a photojournalist. Doing a little investigation."

"Oh yeah? You ever do anything I'd know?"

"The Philadelphia prison riot?" he suggested.

"Uh... nah."

Alan slumped a bit. "Trent Street performing a Brittany Spears song."

"You recorded that? Wow..."

"So, any news in the area? Anything, I don't know, *dangerous* going on?"

"Uh... Not so much around here. Of course, things are pretty safe in this area. In this *exact* area anyway. It's sort of a weird part of town. You go a block that way? Watch your back. You go a block that way and you're in a pretty well-to-do part of down. Darn near everyone who lives over on the next block works down in DC."

Alan cleared his throat. "Okay. Thanks. You've been a big help." He leaned forward, hunching over his meal and dragging Blot out into the open again.

"Chu-chu is spooked. I think they took a swipe at him or something," Blot said. "Which is weird, because it's usually the other way around when he gets around other Shades."

"Did you hear what the waiter said?"

"That there's a whole neighborhood of people who work in your nation's capital? Yes, I heard. If I was still in the business of finding influential hosts, this seems like an awfully good stepping stone to people with political power and/or military power."

"Agreed. No doubt we're in the right place."

"So now what?"

"Now I eat this waffle and we figure out what we can do without immediately getting dogpiled by angry Shades."

Jessie got into her squad car and shut the door. It was getting toward the end of her night shift. Soon the sun would rise. She liked to finish off her shift doing her rounds in the car rather than on foot because, quite frankly, this early in the morning one simply didn't encounter as many people on the street, so there was more value in covering more ground.

"All right, Frightful. We'll see how you like this," she said, carefully opening her reusable shopping bag and lifting out a plastic tray of sushi. "I notice you seem to like the raw stuff better than the cooked stuff, and pickings are pretty slim for raw food at this time of day in the big city. But if you like supermarket sushi from the all-night grocer, I think we can make this a routine at least a few nights a week."

She tore the tape securing the lid and revealed six pieces of salmon on beds of rice. In the darkness of the squad car, Frightful made her presence known as little more than a tingle in Jessie's shoulder and a single, unblinking white eye. It was curious how the rikts always seemed to angle themselves such that only one eye was visible. She was beginning to wonder if Frightful even *had* two eyes. While she admired the mysterious thing, the rikt leaned down and pecked once or twice at the salmon. Satisfied it was fleshy enough to be a proper meal, Frightful gulped it down.

"Great!" she said. "You eat the fish, I'll eat the rice." She popped the tangy sushi rice in her mouth. "Now here's what's got me puzzled. And here's why we're sitting here instead of driving around," she said. "It just doesn't make sense to me why they'd leave these ATMs out if they were robbing them. It isn't as though leaving these out makes them seem *less* guilty. Sure, I didn't notice they were specifically spared the crime wave until I took a closer look, but someone was bound to do that, and anything that makes one part of the city stand out against the rest is likely to make people take a closer look. There must be a different reason."

She reached into her jacket and unfolded a sheet of paper. "This is the restock schedule. And that, Frightful, is the guy doing the restock," she said, eying the uniformed man working at the front of the machine. "I don't have them here, but somewhere, available with a subpoena, is a list of every single serial number on the twenty-dollar bills that are being loaded into that particular machine." Frightful snatched another piece of salmon, and Jessie stuffed the rice in her mouth. "So what we know is that there isn't a single 'dirty' twenty in that machine. At least, with regard to this whole chain of robberies. And no one has robbed that machine so far. So here's what we're going to do. We're going to keep our eyes on that machine."

She checked her watch. "At least for the next forty-five minutes. Because I'm not doing overtime for this."

She leaned back in her seat. Both for the comfort of her shadowy pet and to avoid obviously staking out the ATM, she'd parked in as dark a section of the street as she could manage. Over the course of the next forty minutes, she drilled Frightful on a few simple tricks and generally had a one-sided chat. As useful as the rikt was for lifting the blinders on the supernatural world around her, Jessie found herself primarily feeling grateful for the creature for far more mundane reasons.

"It is so nice to have you here. A little bit of company that's always there is a godsend in a career like this one. Let me tell you, Frightful. If you want to feel alone in a crowd, put on a police uniform. Lots of people clam right up when they see you coming. Sometimes you can win them over. Sometimes, that's just how it'll be. It's a weird sort of loneliness."

She reached into her jacket and found another folded sheet of paper, this one in Blot's strangely precise printing. "According to our resident expert, I shouldn't be surprised that you spend all your time hanging out on me. Blot says according to Gladys, rikts in this world lay claim to certain perches and can happily stay motionless on them for *years* if there's nothing else to occupy them. I suppose that's why you're always snacking. You're moving around a lot more than you would be if you'd picked a nice tree or rock to roost on. I hope I'm not running you ragged."

The rikt surveyed her with the same quiet disinterest she usually did, less like something that was listening and more like something that was waiting for an odd sound to stop.

"You're not the *best* conversationalist, I'll say. But you're at least a match for half of the boys back at the station." She pointed. "Are you going to eat that one? I'd hate to let it go to waste."

Frightful looked at the last piece of salmon, then craned her shadowy head to cast it upon the seat rest and stare out the front window. Jessie took that as permission and helped herself.

The creature released a low, threatening squawk.

"Well if you *wanted* it, you should have *said* something," Jessie said.

She glanced up and froze. Frightful wasn't squawking at Jessie. She was squawking at a distant figure approaching the ATM.

"Good eye, Frightful," she said, fetching a pair of binoculars.

She focused on the woman walking up to the ATM. Sure enough, the woman had a Shade. The Shade was rather longer and more twisted than Blot, and was notably casting itself along the ground ahead of the woman, fighting against some quite powerful light to do so. It gave the overall impression of a shadow walking a human like a dog on a leash. The woman had a backpack and a messenger bag. The backpack was bulging full, and the messenger bag was empty. She looked *very* nervous.

The pair stepped up to the ATM, where the woman started tapping at the keypad. To a casual observer, it would have looked like she was just checking her balance or trying to get some cash. But she'd not dipped her card, and the screen was still prompting her to do so. Meanwhile the Shade cast itself along the front of the machine. It slid a hand into the cash slot. It beckoned with its other hand, and the woman subtly held open her messenger bag. The satchel bulged with something that seemed to come from nowhere. Then the Shade reached into the backpack, which became visibly less stuffed. The woman concluded her false interaction once the bag by her side was heavy and the backpack was entirely slack.

Jessie didn't bother trying to take a picture. She didn't have a proper camera, and at this distance, in this light, she wouldn't have known how to take a useful one regardless. That didn't matter. There would be a camera aimed at the ATM that could be checked if there was reason to do so. For now she made a mental note of the general appearance of the woman and the Shade, then waited until they were well clear of the ATM. She stepped out of the squad car and paced toward the ATM.

"Do me a favor and watch my back, would you?" she said softly to Frightful, who absolutely didn't understand.

She reached the ATM and fished out her wallet. One transaction later, she had a crisp new twenty-dollar bill. She waited until she was back in the squad car to pull out her phone and flip through to the contact that it had taken far too long to find earlier that evening.

"Hello, this is Officer Hearst of the Philadelphia PD. I have witnessed some suspicious activity around an ATM. I'll give the address in a moment, but if I were to give you a serial number, could you give me its status in your investigation? Sure, I'll hold..."

"I've changed my opinion of the coffee," Blot said as they turned a corner and she tossed the empty to-go cup from the diner. "Potency is *not* enough. Gotta have *some* eye for quality."

"No argument from me," Alan said. "My mouth tastes like I drank it out of an ashtray. It did its job, though. I used to be tired. Now I'm tired and jittery."

Once they were able to conclude their business at the diner without being tackled to the ground for trying to dine and dash, they'd set off in the general direction of the fleeing figures from earlier. Chu-chu was considerably more reserved now, choosing to remain wrapped about the stone in Alan's pocket and refusing to be coaxed out even with the scrap of sausage Blot had saved for him.

"What do you suppose they have that spooked the rikt?" Blot said. "Chu-chu didn't look hurt, but he's not himself."

"I don't know. But I'm glad it's nearly dawn, so if whatever it is turns out to be a problem for us, we'll have a fighting chance of keeping away from it long enough for it to get pinned by the sun."

The so-called "good neighborhood" filled with DC commuters certainly had the feel of a place that was built for people with deep pockets. The whole section of town had an entirely different vibe to it than the surrounding areas. The place was just that little bit artificial. Houses were a little too clean. Colors were a little too muted. All the local businesses were small chains that were designed to *feel* like mom-and-pop shops.

"Bobby-Joe's Sandwiches—a division of Yum brands," Alan muttered as he peered at the only other all-night business they'd encountered.

It was tiny, part of a recently built mini-mall that had been subdivided into storefronts designed for takeout and delivery rather than actually serving as a traditional restaurant. There were three tables, each two-seaters, and two of them were fully occupied.

"I can see three Shades inside, including the cashier. And I can feel a lot more. They haven't spotted us yet," Blot said. "Lean against that lamppost so I cast myself against the mailbox. I'll keep an eye on things."

He settled against the lamp and instantly got the "you are falling!" sensation of nearly dozing off while upright. "It's been too long since college to be pulling an all-nighter," he muttered.

"Well wake up. We still don't even have a good plan for what we're going to do if this is the place."

"That's because we can't *make* a plan until we know what we're dealing with," Alan said. "And when it comes right down to it, there's only one thing *to* do. We try to find the Dawn's stuff, steal it back, and run away. We already know there's more of them than we can reasonably fight—which would have been true if there were *two* Shades. So the only option available is to sneak in, steal it, and sneak out. And it should be possible, because that stealth spell seems to be working."

"It's working, sure, but they'll still *see* us."

"So we'll have to be old-fashioned sneaky."

"Uh-huh. One Shade left. Two more went in," she said. "That's easy to *say*, but the whole place is smaller than your apartment. There's only so much sneaking that can happen. Hence the need for a plan."

"Okay... so... set off a fire alarm? Make the people clear out?"

"The Shades wouldn't leave. It's too easy to evacuate if something *is* wrong, so they'll stick around to guard anything that's high value. Two more Shades in."

"How about... can we call the cops on the place somehow?"

"I don't know, maybe. Another three just went in."

He furrowed his brow. "That's seven in."

"Yep."

"And did anyone leave?"

"No."

"There were already seven people in there. There isn't *room* for seven more people. Are they slipping in the front and out the back?"

She shut her eyes. "Feels like they're still in there."

"A basement maybe?"

"Maybe."

"And are you feeling any other Shades anywhere?"

"The whole neighborhood is littered with decoys, so it's *really* hard to tell. But this is the only place I feel any motion. For sure motion at this scale."

"So that's that. This is the best-defended place in the whole city regarding actual Shades, and there's got to be a basement or something. If I was trying to defend a big cache of Dawn's stuff, that's where I'd hide it. So we find a place to stay for a few hours, make sure we're not followed, then come in here during the day, get in, you gather up all the stuff, and we run like our lives depend upon it. So, what? The cop idea? We figure out how to get the place raided?"

"The problem with all your ideas is you're coming up with *human* ideas," she said.

"Call it a limitation, but I *am* a human, so that's kind of what's going to happen."

"All your ideas will get all the regular humans out of the building and leave the Shades. We need something that's the opposite, and... uh-oh..."

"What is it now?" he asked.

"Go. Just go. Walk, but walk fast, right away from the restaurant and don't look back."

Alan tried to obey. The severity of Blot's tone was a kick in the brain, jolting him awake like a blaring alarm, with all the nerve-rattling anxiety that comes with it. But there are few instructions the human mind is less capable of following than "don't look now."

He turned, sweeping the area around the restaurant until his eyes settled on a figure that managed to both stand out from and fade into the world around him. He was a formidable man, just a little taller and a little beefier than the average man on the street, but his stance was slouched and withdrawn in a way that robbed him of size. He was bigger than he looked. He looked familiar, too. But his face looked wrong. His eyes had an unmistakable severity to them, but elsewhere, something was missing.

Alan's eyes widened and he turned away. "That's *Brink*," he hissed.

"Brink? The heavy from the Dawn?" Blot said. "Oh, that's even worse..."

"Even worse than *what*?"

"Did you see his shadow?"

Alan pressed his palm to his forehead. "He had a Shade, didn't he?"

"Not just *a* Shade, Alan. That was Dun."

Alan's heart raced in his chest. Cold drops of sweat poured down his neck. He controlled his breathing, hoping that if he did so for long enough, he could avoid spilling some decent waffles and some bad coffee all over the street of a very nice neighborhood.

"A member of the Dawn who I thought got killed because of limitations we set on the prison mission has been taken as a host by the Shade who I'd *hoped* was killed during that mission," he said.

"Just keep walking," Blot said.

He felt dizzy. His foot missed the curb and he pitched aside. Rather than trying to stop him, Blot darted up and just yanked him down into the shadows with her without warning. The pair whisked along the surface of the streets, pushed this way and that by streetlights and headlights until they were a few blocks from where he'd parked his car. It was at that point that Alan's unprepared body made it utterly clear that the high-speed dive through the shadows was over.

She released him, and he bobbed up into reality in an alley. He made it two stumbling steps forward, struck the edge of a Dumpster, and immediately made excellent use of it.

"Yeah... my sentiments exactly," Blot said, wincing and looking away.

CHAPTER 5

An hour later, Alan was stalking back and forth in the sort of small hotel room that would rent a room to a man for four hours. He should have been sleeping. Everything from his shaking hands and his sagging eyelids made that abundantly clear. But it turned out that horrifying revelations and their resultant doses of adrenaline were much better than caffeine at pushing back the tide of sleep deprivation.

"How can the Shades and the Dawn be working together?!" Alan said. "How can that happen?!"

"It isn't the Shades and the Dawn working together. It's the Shades acquiring a member of the Dawn," Blot said. "And it's precisely a part of our training. For as long as we've known there were powers aligned against us, we've been developing plans to subvert them the same way we subvert anyone. I'm just surprised they managed it. Though if anyone in that prison could, it was Dun."

"We have to tell the old man. The old man from the Dawn. Does he have a name?" Alan shook his head. "It doesn't matter if he does or he doesn't. He needs to know. This explains so much."

"It explains *everything*," Blot said. "But what good does it do to tell them *now*? What are they going to do, tell us some secret technique to defeat one of their best fighters? Are they going to get him to *unknow* things so he'll stop leaking?"

"Well, no. But they'll know who the leak is."

There was a polite knock at the door.

"Now is not the time, whoever you are," Alan shouted.

"Open the door," came the equally polite instruction from the other side.

The request, despite having no force behind it, struck Alan like a two-by-four to the head. He marched to the door, undid both locks, and threw it open. Angel, with their unpleasantly cheerful face, stepped inside. They shut the door behind them.

"I understand you have made the Brink discovery," Angel said.

"The Brink discovery," Alan growled. "You already *knew*?"

"Naturally. Though we are, of course, only human, we do take an interest in such things. I recognize you were sent here under the auspices of reacquiring the Dawn's equipment, but from our point of view, the actual unbalancing element was the joining of the skills and knowledge of a seasoned member of the Dawn with the skills and knowledge of a seasoned member of the Shades and, more importantly, the fact that the union of those two entities was not immediately terminated."

"Immediately terminated, as in Brink didn't kill himself," Alan said.

"Quite so. Overwhelmingly that is the outcome that has occurred in circumstances such as this. To rise to the level within the Dawn that Brink has requires undergoing an unimaginable amount of indoctrination. If the Dawn can be characterized as a cult, and I'm not sure it strictly fits the definition, then Brink has risen to the second-highest level achievable within it. He has been exposed to their most sophisticated methods of mental fortification."

"Brainwashing," Blot muttered, unheard by Angel.

"He would absolutely, without a doubt, consider his own life to be a small price to pay for the elimination of any Shade," Angel continued. "Let alone one of such a high level of skill and influence as Dun. That he didn't suggests he may have somehow been persuaded to willingly work with them. And that can only lead to the inevitable fall of the Dawn, taking with it the balance that we so thoroughly seek to maintain. And so, now that you have confirmed both the identity and location, the task I expect of you is simple. End this partnership should the hint of an opportunity arise."

"Oh," Alan said with exasperation. "Is that all?"

"It will not be simple. I realize that. But on the bright side, it may *also* be unavoidable, as I must imagine that the Brink-Dun union will be quite dedicated to keeping hold of their stolen gear. Also, I find it notable that *Dun* acquired a member of the Dawn. The two words are so similar. Interesting."

"I refuse to believe that someone who finds that interesting is intellectually capable of dominating us with their words..." Blot said.

"I've been given permission to linger long enough to provide some insight, should you require it."

"No!" Blot snapped. "Make them leave."

"But first, permit me to prepare some refreshment," Angel said.

Alan took a seat and waited for them to do precisely that, because the wording made any other action impossible.

Jessie yawned and rolled out of bed. It had only been about four hours since she'd gone to bed, but by the nature of her inconsistent shifts since getting back into fieldwork, she'd gotten into the habit of sleeping for four hours at a time with a gap in the middle. That allowed for adjusting to just about any schedule by sliding one of the four-hour chunks around. It wasn't ideal. If she kept it up for more than a few weeks, she found she'd get terribly irritable. But for now she considered it to be worth the discomfort if it meant guaranteeing she could stay off desk work for a while.

It *also* meant she could check in with the station to see if her little investigation had borne fruit. She dialed an internal number of a friend of hers at the station who was *much* happier working a desk than she was.

"Jessie Girl!" he said.

"Hey Buddy!" she said. "I *seem* to remember telling you that if anyone ever heard you call me that, I'd stop bringing you muffins whenever our shifts line up. I don't want that catching on as a nickname."

"Relax, I'm alone. What's up? You on your way in? Cranberry walnut," he said.

"No, no. I'm doing late shifts right now. But I called in a serial number last night and dropped it off with the financial crimes guys before—"

"That was you? Boy, Jessie Girl, you've got this place hopping."

"Have I?

"The bank got back to us quick. Are you going to be able to swear an affidavit that you got that twenty where you got it and when you got it?"

"Of course."

"Good. Because that thing wasn't in the stack that was loaded into that machine a few minutes prior. It wasn't *supposed* to be, anyway. It was stolen from another ATM around eight hours earlier. Figure *that* one out."

"Wild," she said, her mind already putting the pieces together.

"Yeah, it's a mess. They're launching an investigation into the armored truck company. The whole chain of custody is being interrogated. A real mess. A *real* mess. Are you going to head down here to get that done?"

"If they need me, I will, but my shift isn't until the evening."

"Oh, don't donate your time to the station. Take it from me, you make them pay top dollar."

"Certainly."

"Plus it's going to be a *load* of paperwork. I'll be out of here by then, though. So... cranberry walnut."

"I'm aware of your order, Bud," she said. "See you then."

She hung up the phone and trudged to the kitchen. A gentle tingle on her shoulder heralded the arrival of her pet/roommate.

"Just in time, Frightful," she said. "I'm not a detective, and I wasn't really seeking that particular career track. But I do seem to have cracked my first case." She opened the refrigerator and pulled out some eggs and clicked on the stove. "The Shades are paying their bills, or at least a large portion of the bills I've been able to check up on without violating civil liberties, with cash. And we already know they can just *get* money from machines. But the money they've been getting from the machines hasn't been hot, so they haven't been tripping any of the automatic safeguards. Which means either the money is legitimate, or it has been laundered."

She smeared some butter on the pan. "If I got a hot twenty out of a machine that was just loaded with clean ones, it's unreasonable for the folks at the station to think anything other than some sort of a scheme where the bank or some member of the staff that restocks the machines is running a money laundering scheme. But *we* know that if the Shades can empty an ATM, they can just as easily *fill* an ATM. It's honestly pretty brilliant. Steal money from one place, then steal money from another place and replace it with the dirty money. By replacing it, there's no sign the second theft happened, and thus the second collection of bills stays clean."

She cracked an egg. "It's extra genius, because it requires, basically, magic powers to do it. And as we've established, the legal system wasn't devised with magic in mind. So even knowing this with near certainty doesn't really get us any closer to solving the case. On one hand, it eases my conscience about suspecting and investigating them, because now it's not just me assuming that they're doing bad because they're Shades, it's me having a credible reason to suspect they're conspiring to launder money. But it *also* puts me in a position where I can't realistically investigate them, because they're using 'impossible' means to do it."

Frightful endured the labyrinthine intricacies of the legal system with her usual disinterest.

"As an aside," Jessie said. "Do you like eggs, and do you prefer them cooked or not?" She held up a raw egg. "Treats?"

Frightful leaned forward and took the egg's shadow in her beak so gently the shell didn't even crack. Then, a dart of her head, and it vanished. The rikt fluffed her feathers and squawked happily.

"Don't get too used to them. They're not the cheapest treat. But I'll keep them in mind when you're extra good." She carefully converted the egg from sunny-side up to over easy. "So here's the puzzle. How do you prove there is a ring of money launderers doing their thing when 'their thing' is something that no one should actually be able to do? I can't justify an investigation into that apartment building. Even if the person who did the money swap is on camera, the Shade won't be. And either there isn't an internal mechanism in the ATM that detects that sort of thing, or they learned not to trip it. So the proper investigation would certainly be into the people filling the ATM, and I've got to believe the chain of custody will clear them. So it'll be a dead end."

She plated the egg and loaded some toast into the toaster oven. "I don't like it, but I don't think we're going to see justice without stretching the law. I'm going to need to put pressure on someone. Find an informant." She huffed a frustrated breath. "Either way I'm going to have to talk to some people I *really* hoped I'd never have to talk to again."

Angel, displaying a level of delight that suggested it was a novelty, operated the motel room's coffee machine.

"I'm not sharing my good coffee pods with them," Blot said.

"You have good coffee pods?" Alan said.

"No!" Angel said brightly, assuming the comment was for them. "Loose tea leaves. I have a bit of a weakness for a good Darjeeling."

The Glint slung their messenger bag around in front of them and fished out a metal tin and a small plastic bag with an odd circular cage about the size of a golf ball inside. They loaded the cage with leaves with the methodical care of an Old West sheriff rolling a cigarette in a black-and-white movie.

"We've had our concerns about a willing collaboration between the Dawn and the Shades for some time. And those concerns have been somewhat deepened by the simple fact that things aren't progressing as we had anticipated. A scenario such as this should have been followed almost immediately by the open slaughter of the Dawn. Hardly a desirable outcome, but at least an expected one. Our assessment at this point is that they are moving with greater than expected caution. Perhaps because of your own highly effective intervention in the past. Perhaps because our own actions combined with yours have reduced their capacity to the point that they doubt they will be able to overcome the Dawn without first rendering them *entirely* toothless. But regardless, we cannot depend upon much further delay. The next action must be ours."

"Now when you say 'ours,' I don't suppose that means you're going to march into the sandwich shop, which you must have watched us investigate, instruct them to hand over the Dawn stuff, and be done with it?" Alan said.

"Ah. Yes, I suppose 'ours' was an imprecise bit of language. I meant, of course, yours. Direct intervention like that is something we prefer to avoid," they said.

"Yeah. I prefer to avoid it too. But apparently *I* don't have a *choice*. Because everyone knows where I live and likes to dangle the safety of me and my friends in front of me like both the carrot and the stick. You could solve this all *now*. Why don't you?"

"It is simply not our way. Trust me. It is better this way."

"Trust them," Blot scoffed.

"I am willing to offer advice, if you like," Angel said.

"I'm all ears."

"As there is now a very real and immediate need to end the collaboration between Brink and his Shade, there is no reasonable outcome that doesn't end in at least *some* bloodshed. But I understand your distaste for violence. I share it."

"Hence your policy of getting *other* people to do the violence *for* you," Alan said.

"If you didn't say it, I would have," Blot said.

"Precisely!" Angel said brightly, as though there was no issue whatsoever with that arrangement. "And to our great good fortune, you can utilize a similar policy. The Dawn has extensive procedures, methodologies, and contingencies regarding how best to deal with situations of this nature. All of them, naturally, end in the elimination of the compromised party. My recommendation is simply to reacquire the stolen equipment, hand it over to the Dawn, and direct them at the concentration of Shades centered upon Dun and Brink. You needn't get any blood on your hands."

"You and I have very different ideas about who is culpable for a given bit of murder," Alan said.

"You are free to pursue different methods, but I cannot overstate the necessity of success. I will say, however, that it would behoove you to act quickly if your goal is to have the Dawn take care of Dun rather than you. As, if our oversight can be trusted, at this very moment Dun is departing the city for parts unknown. If you act before his return, you might dodge the entire issue."

They brewed their tea. Alan glanced at Blot.

"What do we think?" he said.

"I think every single thing these things ask us to do makes me want to follow their orders even less. But I also think it's suspicious that they're *asking* us to do this," she said.

Alan glanced at Angel. "Blot points out that you're not just commanding us to get this done."

"Quite so. We have observed that you seem to operate best when given a degree of latitude. I would suggest you take pains not to abuse this privilege."

"The privilege of *free will*?"

"Yes!" Angel said, again not offering so much as a suggestion of shame or even self-awareness. "But I've taken enough of your time. I'll run along. The others have requested I do some specialized research that could come in handy depending upon the outcome of this endeavor. Good luck to you. As always, we will be watching." They stepped out the door and shut it behind them.

"Angel stole the motel's coffee mug," Blot observed.

"I'm surprised this place even supplied coffee mugs in the first place." Alan shook his head and flopped onto the bed. "Are we ever going to be done with this?"

"We'll figure it out. The gear has to be in the basement, right, so—"

"Not just that, *this*," Alan said, waving his arms. "All of it. Supernatural supervisors showing up at the door and giving us little errands that, oh, by the way, will lead to murders. Lingering on someone's hit list and having 'safety' defined by how well we can hide and how many bigger fish they need to fry first? Is this ever going to be over?"

"Alan, you're focusing on the end of the race when we really need to be focusing on the next step."

"I'm tired of running a race, Blot! I was starting to come unraveled when all I had to worry about was getting enough photos sold to pay my bills. Now financial ruin is way down at the bottom of a tottering heap of bigger concerns that will crush not just me but everyone I know, and might take the whole *world* with it."

"I know, Alan. I know. I'm here with you. I'm in this. All we can do is survive."

Alan sat up. "But can we survive? That's the question here. If you just focus on the next step, you might miss that every single one of them is leading us to a cliff."

He felt a tap on his shoulder and snapped around. It was Blot in what he'd come to think of as her dream form, which was paradoxically what she probably *really* looked like—impish, dressed in rags, with hair fluttering as if caught in an unseen breeze. The room was also *wrong* somehow. Still a motel room, but not the one he knew he was in. Just *a* motel room, some sort of default mash-up of every place he'd ever stayed, complete with a painting on his wall that was *actually* a painting from the sewing room at his grandmother's house.

"Did I fall asleep?" he said.

"The instant your head hit the bed. You were really tired," Blot said.

"Thank heaven for exhaustion, I guess. If it was up to my mind, I'd have been racing in circles for another few hours."

"If it was up to me, I wouldn't have done the whole 'pop in and have a word with you' thing for a while. Let you get a real bit of sleep. But this was your choice, not mine."

"I lucidly dreamed on my own, on purpose?" he said.

"Congratulations on the new skill, I suppose," she said.

"I guess I felt I needed to get this figured out before I could rest," he said.

"Yeah. Or else you're afraid of what your mind would throw at you if it was left to its own devices. I've gotten a glimpse at what's behind these walls as you were sort of imagining them into place. Let's just say we won't be answering that door if anyone knocks."

"Great... At least Chu-chu can't come in here," he said.

"What do you have against Chu-chu? He's a little darling and he's being *so* good right now. You should see him. Tucked in the shadow of his little rock. He's still *really* tense, though. Tenser now than he was a few minutes ago. I wish I knew what it was that spooked him..."

"I'm sure whatever it is, we'll run into it at the worst possible time." He covered his face. "At least this whole mess has finally established one thing as an incontestable truth. Fate does *not* have a plan. Because no universe that was being run properly would have put *me* in the position to be one of humanity's only lines of defense against the more maniacal members of your kind."

Blot huffed a frustrated breath. "Alan. Not that I'm not just chomping at the bit to pat you on the head and tell you everything will be okay, but you've got to stop with this 'why is this happening to me' nonsense."

"I know it's happening to you too."

"It's happening to *everyone*. The guy at the front desk who gave us the room? It's happening to him. That lady fighting with the key to get through the door two rooms over? It's happening to her, too. This is happening to everyone. To the entire *world*. And that goes for the other Shades, too. There are maybe *three* Shades who are doing what they're doing because they *want* to be doing it. Everyone else is doing it because they've been taught to believe it's something they *should* want to do, or because they don't have a choice. If you want to mope about how awful it all is, and how you can't handle it, then that's fine. That we can't handle it alone is the whole idea. The *point* is to overwhelm. But we're in a very big club when it comes to beings who have been swept up in the flood that's dragging us toward a waterfall. We just have the benefit of *knowing the waterfall is there*. Is there fate? I don't know. I don't care. It wouldn't make a difference if there was or there wasn't. But *something* put us in a position to be able to make some choices about what we do, and every moment we sit here and tug at the unraveling threads of our lives is another moment of precious insight that's been squandered. Remember, if Angel can be trusted—and I'm not convinced they can—then we've got a window where we *might* not face Dun/Brink when we do this.

"And, may I say, one of these days I'd like to be the one having the mental collapse. Yes, I was technically trained and prepared for this. I was one of the things behind the curtain that you've unwillingly been given the ability to look behind. But I was trained, and prepared, to be *fodder*. And at least this is still your world, for now. At least you have family and friends. You have a lot to lose, sure. But when it all comes down to it, that means you still have a lot. I'm aware that I'm lucky to have both you, a host who treats me like a person instead of either a kidnapper or a parasite, and Chu-chu, an adorable little drop of midnight who can do no wrong. And if things keep going the way they're going, I'll have to share... No, you know what? Let's keep that can of worms sealed for the moment."

She crossed her arms and huffed again. "Now do you need a few more minutes to wring yourself out, or can we start figuring out how we're going to paddle toward the shore before the next big drop?"

Alan flexed his fingers a few times, admiring how somehow he'd been able to carry over his achiness from reality, then turned to her. "Am I in a comfortable position out there? Or am I going to have a crick in my neck when I wake up?"

She shut her eyes, then waggled her hand. "I don't think you'd *choose* to fall asleep lying like that, but you don't look too contorted."

"Good enough. I'd rather stay asleep than have to risk not getting back to sleep. Let's see if I can dream up a guess at the layout of the sandwich shop and start planning."

It took what felt like an hour to properly conjure up something resembling the proper layout of the sandwich shop. Alan was new to the idea of sculpting his own dreams, and it was quite clear that dreams weren't really a place where precision and accuracy were simple to come by. But Blot had been able to use his phone to fill in some gaps, and now they were looking at as near to perfect a simulation of the sandwich shop itself as they were likely to get.

"So," Alan said, gazing at the mental construct. "Two doors to the shop itself. Front and back. And this thing here on the street is probably a direct hatch leading to the basement." He experimentally opened the hatch, but in the dream, it just led to solid ground beneath. "There seriously are *no* pictures of the basement?"

"None that I could find. Though searching this up on your phone isn't very pleasant. I'm already tired of having to have fingers. You should dig out your laptop. I can type on the shadows of the keys a lot more easily," Blot said.

As Alan stared at the solid ground, it slowly started to rumble and slide, emptying into a basement that almost certainly didn't match the real one at all, but would be a reasonable stand-in. He slammed the hatch and stepped into the shop, where he found the one door that they couldn't match up with a storage closet or other room. He opened it, and an assumed staircase dropped down into the recently imagined basement.

"All right. So we know the clerk has a Shade. And we know that most of the patrons have Shades." He tapped a door. "This is the employee-only area, and this is the bathroom. I have to assume the employee-only area is going to be filled with other Shades as well."

"Might also be a good place for the gear to hide, though," Blot observed.

"True. We've got the industrial fridge over here, griddles over there." He rubbed his face. "This is going to have the highest Shades-per-square foot in the world, and I already can barely walk around in it without sidling to get past counters and stuff. We had a whole *office building* to run and hide in when we first faced some Shades and we barely survived."

"Sure, but we're more skilled now," Blot said. "Though we've got to assume *they* will be, too. I don't think fighting is going to get us anywhere. Especially if they have a heap of Dawn weapons. I wouldn't put it past a well-trained Shade to use an anti-Shade weapon on an enemy Shade. And a dagger is a dagger. Silver and magic or not, if they ram it through you, you'll die all the same."

"Trust me, I'm well aware. So fighting is out. That leaves stealth, I suppose."

She counted off on her fingers. "Stealth, misdirection, intimidation, bluffing. We've got options, and they just so happen to be entirely my specialties."

"Then lead the way. But one thing I think can't be argued—we're going to need a plan B."

"I'm not stopping before plan F. So here's what I'm thinking for A—"

Chapter 6

After a few hours of errands and a second nap of four hours or so, Jessie was back on the beat. She'd spent most of her waking time since learning of the money laundering ring operating right under her nose to steel herself for what some of her fellow officers would have had no problem at all doing. She was going to put pressure on someone.

Finding a target was easy enough. All she had to do was wait in front of the apartment building with Frightful curled in her shadow and watch for the evening sun to cast a Shade on the ground. It took very little time before a skittish young man, maybe in his early twenties, marched out with the sort of skip and trot in his gait that suggested someone was urging him to hurry. She lengthened her stride to keep pace across the street and, when the time was right, dashed across.

"Excuse me, sir! Sir," she called, with a precisely calibrated balance of friendliness and authority in her tone.

It caused him to make a panicked change in direction, clearly aiming for a dimly lit alleyway. But his body hadn't quite gotten the message about the change of route with enough time for him to make the shift cleanly and he stumbled. She was able to catch him by the arm and straighten him up. She didn't let go once he was steady. His shadow roughly matched him, though there was a jitter to its outline, like it was flexing a muscle to appear so.

"Careful, sir," she said. "You wouldn't want to get hurt."

"I-is there something wrong, Officer?" he said.

She gave his shadow a very pointed look, then looked back at him. "I think we both know the answer to that question."

"She sees us, you fool!" hissed the Shade, eyes shooting open. "Get into the darkness."

"I really, really wouldn't wrench your arm out of my grip and run for the shadows right now, sir," she said, trying to appear as intimidating as she could.

It wasn't a strength, but it kept the man from bolting.

"Wise choice," she said. "I've been doing some investigation regarding the residents of the apartment building I just saw you leave, and I wonder if you'd be willing to aid in the investigation."

"Don't say a *word*," the Shade barked.

"I-I don't know what you're talking about," the man said.

"Sir. May I ask your name?" she said.

"You will say *nothing*," the Shade growled.

"It has been discovered that money taken from ATMs in the outer sections of the city has been swapped for the contents of ATMs in the vicinity of your apartment building. I personally observed a"—she glanced at the shadow again—"*similarly equipped* young woman interact with a freshly loaded ATM, and following that interaction, the ATM was filled entirely with stolen money. That is money laundering, you realize. And because they are acts committed as a part of an ongoing criminal enterprise, that makes it racketeering. Law enforcement has significant tools at its disposal to deal with racketeers."

"I'm... I didn't—" the man began.

"*Silence,*" the Shade hissed.

"I'm going to ask you to be reasonable. Think about this with clarity and logic. When the time comes to prosecute, those who cooperate will come out much more favorably. And those who cooperate *early* might come out of it clean."

"She cannot prove *anything*. You will keep your mouth *shut* or I will make you regret it. Do you hear me? *Do you?*" the Shade raved.

Jessie took a breath and addressed the shadow directly, keeping her voice low and trying to cheat her eye line such that onlookers wouldn't find themselves wondering why an officer was talking to a man's shadow. "I know for a fact that many of you are coerced into this position. You are operating out of fear. You've been here long enough that you know half of what you've been told doesn't apply anymore. You don't have to go along with any criminal action set forth by your superiors."

There was the briefest flicker in the Shade's expression, an instant that belied a desperate desire for a way out of the cage that had been built for them. In any other situation, Jessie would have latched onto that, kept the suspect cornered and talking until the deep-down desire to do right, or at least to stop doing wrong, could come to the surface. Many, many times she'd encountered people who were breaking the law for lack of other options. Overwhelmingly she'd been able to nudge them toward help or a way out that they'd convinced themselves didn't exist. But there was no chance for that here. The level of distrust between half of the public and the police was a steep obstacle to overcome. The level of distrust between a Shade and a human was insurmountable.

The desperation of both man and Shade was rising to an unsustainable level. The man started to pull at the grip on his arm. The Shade reached a set of lengthening claws toward her, fighting the sun as best he could until needle-sharp tips were threatening to scrape her boots.

Something about that motion, about the physical threat, caused Frightful to stir and rumble with a half squawk. The sound caused the man to flinch and the Shade's eyes to widen. It broke the dark being's concentration, knocking it back to matching the man's posture.

"What was that?" the Shade said, his tone making it clear he knew precisely what it was but was hoping he was wrong.

Jessie allowed the faintest of smiles to curve her lips as the piece of a new plan fell into place. She wasn't much for intimidation, especially when the law wasn't quite on her side. This sort of situation called for a liberal application of good cop, bad cop. But she was only one woman, and she'd gone her entire career trying to *avoid* being a bad cop, so she was out of practice. But maybe there was a bad cop waiting in the wings after all.

"I'll tell you what, sir. The sun is awfully bright. Maybe you'd be more comfortable in the shade," she said.

She stepped in front of him and backed into the darkened alleyway, still gripping his arm. As she slipped into the shadow of the building, Frightful rose up from her shadow to take her proper place on Jessie's shoulder. The rikt emerged with her eye fixed in a piercing, angry glare at the human and Shade. Her posture was stiff and threatening. But not nearly as threatening as the low, croaking squawk. Frightful did *not* like these two.

"What the hell is that?" the man said, now trying to tug free to *avoid* going into the darkness.

"That is a rikt. How did a human get a *rikt*?" the Shade said, showing roughly the same level of terror as one would expect from a human if Jessie had a snarling Rottweiler straining at its leash.

"Please, please," Jessie said. "Keep your voice down. Frightful is quite well trained, but I wouldn't want you to spook her. I suppose you haven't heard of the pilot program within the force. We try not to publicize it. Best the public doesn't know about Shades just yet. But if you're going to be a part of society, you're going to have to obey society's laws. I'm confident Shades are every bit as civic-minded as humans. But like humans, sometimes they need to be reminded of what lines not to cross. So I'm the first of a small but elite group of rikt handlers on the force. Think of us as a K-9 unit, but a bit more two-dimensional and avian."

"No," the Shade said. "Such a beast would never obey a human…"

Jessie could feel she was teetering on the cusp of the Shade's willing-ness to call her bluff. After a silent prayer that her time trying to train Frightful hadn't been wasted, she eyed a trash can beside her suspect. She shifted the shoulder Frightful was perched on and pointed.

"Go!" she said.

Frightful hesitated for a moment, then darted to the shadow of the trash can. The hefty rikt struck the can's shadow with enough force to tip it aside, causing a startling clash of the lid bouncing off and some aluminum cans spilling out. The moment Frightful left her, she could no longer see the Shade. She slapped her arm.

"Come!" she said.

Two heart-stopping seconds later, she felt the sting of Frightful's claws, and the terrified, cowering form of the Shade became visible again. Jessie pulled a stick of jerky from her pocket and held it up.

"Treats, Frightful," she said.

The creature tore a hunk of the meat off and gulped it down.

"Wh-what? I don't understand. What *is* that?" the man asked.

"A revolutionary next step in law enforcement. Now please. If you could provide some help on the subject of the suspected money laundering, the Philadelphia Police Department would be quite grateful."

The man looked at his shadow.

"What... other commands does it know?" the shadow said, unwilling to look away from the rikt.

"Oh. I really don't think you want me to demonstrate. She's not quite so easy to call back from some of the other commands," Jessie said. "And please. No sudden movements. She's got a bit of a hair trigger when it comes to fleeing suspects."

"What sort of information do you require?" the Shade said. "And what sort of protection can you provide?"

"We can discuss both of those questions back at the station. Follow me."

Alan stared down the sandwich shop. Raw exhaustion combined with a *lot* of plotting and planning meant that it was nearly sunset by the time they actually started. Alan had hoped they would get started a little closer to noon to perhaps take the edge off the powers that could be arrayed against them, but Blot convinced him moving forward with the sun low in the sky would give *her* the greatest chance of being helpful. The sandwich shop was just close enough to the general milling about that came with a street festival to make it a little too dangerous to try anything they had in mind until the crowds had started to thin out. And, as it so happened, the low sun was indispensable for the plan that they'd settled upon for plan A. So they'd burned the remaining time preparing for their alphabet of different plans, which had included such diverse and nonsensical tasks as finding a specific energy drink, buying some cheap key chains, picking up some white enamel paint, and selecting a good, sturdy rubber ball. He'd also bought a bandanna to tie around his face, as he *really* didn't want to be recognized if things went south.

"Remember, hyperventilate or whatever. We need you holding your breath *good and long* if this is going to work," Blot said.

Alan nodded and started taking deep breaths. This was an east-west street, and they were a fair distance along the road, with the setting sun behind them. They were crouched beside a soda machine, barely in its shadow. Blot reached into Alan's pocket and revealed the stone with Chu-chu wrapped around it, then produced the brown rubber ball.

"We have a new game for you, Chu-chu. I just know you're going to do great." She eased her shadowy finger out of the darkness and etched a rune on the ball, matching the one on the stone that Chu-chu called home. "Now, this is going to be a little scary, but scary things are fun, right?" Blot said. "And I promise I'll give you the very, *very* best treat we can find. Plus, you'll get to do some chasing. You *love* chasing."

She handed Alan the stone. He placed it on top of the soda machine.

"Chu-chu! Chu-chu-chu!" Blot said sweetly, waggling the ball.

The sprite form of the rikt peeled off the sunny rock and coiled about the ball.

"All right. Again. This'll be fun. Just do what comes naturally and come back to the stone here and we'll give you so many pets and goodies, all right?"

"Are we *absolutely* sure this will work?" Alan asked.

"Near enough," Blot said.

She gave the curled-up rikt a scratch. Alan could have sworn he heard a beep when she did it.

"What was that?" he said.

"Deep breath," she replied.

Alan nodded, quite accustomed to not getting answers. She handed the ball to Alan, then eased her arms out and grasped him under his arms. He sucked in a breath. She yanked him and the ball into the shadows, then the group slid out into the sunlight.

The sharp angle of the light pushed them along the street at a maddening pace. They wove between the shadows of crab lovers loitering in the streets, trying to decide where they were going to eat. The several blocks separating them vanished in the blink of an eye.

"Coming up fast. Everyone hold on," Blot said, her white eyes settling upon the shadow of a parking meter. "Now!"

Blot released Alan with one arm and grabbed hold of the shadow of the parking meter. Alan, for an instant, bobbed partially into three dimensions again. It was a split second, but long enough to hurl the rubber ball Chu-chu was curled about with all the momentum of their multiblock slide. The ball whistled through the open doorway and pinballed around the interior, startling all inside, while Blot and Alan pulled entirely into the shadows again and surfed the light through the window to huddle down in the corner of the shop amid the chaos the ball caused. The two normal humans dashed out of the shop, one of them covered with the remnants of an iced tea that had been upset by the bouncing ball. A small crowd immediately started to form, attracted by the commotion.

Chu-chu, evidently unwilling to ride the ball as it careened around the shop, uncoiled from it and launched to a bottle of ketchup on one of the tables, sliding it off and smashing it before bounding to and fro on his own chaotic trajectory. Once it was clear to the Shades inside that a rikt had burst upon their little hideout, a fresh wave of chaos erupted as orders were barked at human hosts and the Shades did their best to subdue Chu-chu, unaware of the rikt's savant-level skill when it came to avoiding capture if it had something more interesting to do. And right now that more interesting thing was to nip and harass the Shades. The low-grade distrust and irritation Chu-chu showed for other Shades seemed to convince the rikt to make up for lost time and really give these Shades something to worry about.

The multilevel chaos was precisely what Blot and Alan needed. Doors flew open, humans and Shades flooded out to aid in the rikt hunt like clowns finally unloading from their car. In the madness, a single shadow without an obvious owner was too small a detail to be considered.

Alan felt his body beginning to demand a fresh breath of air. Blot navigated along beneath the tables and, finally, slipped beneath the basement door after it slammed. The basement had been completely emptied in the madness, and the lights were, of course, not just switched off but free of bulbs. Blot released Alan, and he popped up at the base of the stairs.

"That went... pretty well," he gasped quietly, fumbling a headlamp on and switching it to its dimmest setting.

The headlamp was the latest addition to his growing collection of "Shade mission gear." It cost nearly two hundred dollars but was apparently tested to be just short of bulletproof, with a strap so secure he worried it would cut off circulation to his brain.

He climbed the stairs and clicked the lock for the door, for all the good it would do.

"It should be child's play to find the Dawn gear. We're inside the building, which should put us behind any wards to hide them. And there are Shards of Shadow. Those things resonate with power. I should be able to find them... in..." She trailed off as she darted about among the crates and boxes.

"Something wrong?" Alan whispered, joining the search and glancing nervously toward the stairs at every thump and shout from above.

"I don't... I don't feel the shards down here. They couldn't have warded these boxes, could they?" Blot said.

Every moment they were out of shadow, Alan's anxiety ratcheted higher. Things were certainly still chaotic up there. An alarm had started blaring, and water was pouring out from beneath the door. He rummaged through a row of winter coats, flipping open boxes. There were napkins, sauce packets, cleaning supplies. All sorts of stuff necessary to run a sandwich shop but nothing silver or enchanted.

"I'm not sure we're in the right place," Alan said. "Surely they would have left someone down here to guard it. We had a whole step to the plan for dealing with that."

"Where else could they *be*?! Unless the Dawn was wrong and this isn't the place."

Alan knocked two more winter coats from where they'd been hung on the corners of a wire shelf. "Wait..." he said. "It's like seventy-five degrees out. Why are there so many coats down here..."

"Now's not the time for curiosity, Alan. Now's the time for searching."

Alan felt one of the coats and found something blocky in the pocket. "This one has a cell phone in the pocket. With charge. Someone was using this coat today." He narrowed his eyes. "We have to get back up there."

"Once we're up, we need to get out fast. Remember, they had something to spook Chu-chu away when he tried to chase them last night. He might already be gone up there."

"I don't think we're going to find the stuff down here. But I think I know where it is. Sneak us up there and find someplace where it's safe to bob me back up."

"I'll try..."

He took another breath and she yanked him down. Sliding up and around each step on the way up was terribly disorienting, somehow more so than on the way down. They slipped beneath the door to find that Chu-chu must have *really* been enjoying tormenting the local Shades, because not only were they still angrily trying to catch him but the gushing water and blaring alarm turned out to be the sprinkler system. It had activated at some point and the restaurant was soaked.

"There's no way we're hiding you, Alan. What's the plan?" Blot asked.

He couldn't answer while still hidden, but he hoped she could interpret his gestures even if he was having a hard time making sense of them while a two-dimensional shape on the floor. He extended his arm, indicating the industrial fridge.

Blot hauled him toward it and attempted to slide up between the seal and the body of the fridge. It may have been a tight seal, but a shadow had no width. She *should* have been able to push through without effort. But it *was* taking effort. A *lot* of it. Arcane measures had been taken to keep Shades out of the fridge.

"Brace yourself. I'm going to have to push hard, but I think I can get through this. It's just going to mean borrowing a little of your oomph."

Alan lacked the capacity to argue in his current state. He felt a strange, wearying draw upon him, like someone had pulled the plug from the drain at the bottom of his spirit and it was slowly starting to swirl away. But it did the job. Like one magnet pushing past another, Blot forced them past the resistance, tumbling them into the refrigerator's interior.

It should have been a cold box the size of a small closet, filled with shelves, lunch meat, and the like. It was not. The interior was impossibly massive. Like some sort of cartoon bank vault, towering dozens of feet tall and stretching easily fifty yards in all directions. This wasn't as simple as a secret door leading into the next storefront or something. This was mystical in nature. This place had been twisted, expanded. Like the hiding place Gladys called home, it was larger than the space that contained it, and like the sandwich shop in Alan's dream, it didn't *quite* match the place it was attempting to mimic. The walls were featureless stretches of stainless steel, with only what Alan imagined were the original shelves of the refrigerator forming a sort of cage between the entrance and the rest of the massive space.

If there was any doubt about this being the proper place, two... *things* were waiting for them. Alan supposed they were a pair of humans with Shades, but the partnership had pushed the humans almost past the point of recognition. They were compact in their form, squat and troglodytic. Long arms and short legs, each so heavily muscled there was some question about their range of motion. Unnatural, huge eyes darted and shifted wildly. These were shifters who had turned their hosts into little, powerful balls of muscle capable of seeing in the near-perfect darkness that Shades preferred. The muscles were tense, eyes locked on the door. They would have been utterly terrifying if not for the slightly comic detail of them both being bundled in ill-fitting winter gear to ward off the cold of the fridge. Meanwhile, their Shades had their own eyes trained on a heap of locked boxes behind them. The oversize eyes shifted and locked on Blot and Alan.

"Ahgh!" croaked one of the shifters, the capacity to speak having not survived the shape change.

"Bright light alone won't work on shifters. So plan D, then," Blot said.

She released Alan, and he sprang somewhat unsteadily back into three dimensions, his headlamp suddenly shedding its light onto the scene. The spiritual "absence of temperature" coldness was replaced by the real thing. The monsters widened their stances, ready to spring. Alan held up his hand, and Blot produced a small white cylinder with a ring dangling from it, placing it in his hand.

"Keep back," Alan said, trying to summon up all of his intensity. "Do you know what this is? This is a flash-bang! I pull this ring and every human—or human *adjacent* thing—ends up blind and deaf for the next twenty minutes, and every Shade in the room gets the mother of all sunburns."

The threat landed roughly as he'd hoped it would with the twisted humans, keeping them in place. But the Shades, alas, knew better.

"He won't set off a weapon like that. It would strike him as well. Attack!"

"They always try to call our bluff," Blot said.

Alan pulled the pin and heaved the grenade. Wisely, the shifters dashed to put as much distance as possible between themselves and the cylinder, which started hissing and spraying as soon as it struck the ground. Unwisely, Alan dashed *toward* it. Practically straddling the weapon in order to tear open the crates that had been left unguarded.

"Bingo," he said.

The crates were filled with silver daggers, stacks of books, boxes that were the precise match for the one that had held the Shard of Shadow they'd encountered back in the prison with Brink, and equipment Alan could only guess at the purpose of.

"I hate this, I hate this, I hate this..." Blot squealed, producing some thick canvas sacks and sweeping up everything that *wasn't* specifically a weapon enchanted to injure her kind.

Alan started loading the anti-Shade weaponry into the sacks so quickly and haphazardly that if the daggers had been properly sharp, he probably would have lost a finger. But the haste was wise, because it wasn't much longer before it became clear to all involved that the scent filling the air from the sputtering can wasn't some sort of chemical igniter about to unleash military intensities of sound and light, and was in fact ginseng, taurine, caffeine, and all sorts of the overhyped chemicals that manufacturers dumped into the energy drink Alan had painted white earlier that day.

Alan had managed to load two bags—about half of the remaining weapons—before a bundle of muscle bounded at him. Blot yanked Alan and the sacks of weapons into the shadows, breathing a brief sigh of relief as she discovered the sack had, as they'd hoped, protected her from the effects of the weapons. The sigh was cut short when the shifter's Shade thumped hard into the pair of them, as slipping into the shadows wasn't much of a defense against another shadow.

The blow sent Alan bounding back out of the shadows, and he slammed into the crates, overturning them and spilling the rest of the goods they'd been sent to collect. Blot desperately contorted herself to avoid being skewered by the things. Alan snatched a silver-tipped stick and climbed to his feet, brandishing it wildly.

"I'll use it! Don't test me!" he raved.

Again the Shades held their hosts back, unwilling to venture too close to the now *very* well-armed Alan. Blot vanished everything that wouldn't actively harm her from the spilled contents, then awkwardly started scooping up daggers and other enchanted silver with the canvas sacks while Alan slashed wildly at the shifters whenever they approached. They quickly determined that a photographer, even a heavily armed one, wasn't likely to be much of a match for them, and they started to approach with violence in their eyes. Worse, the commotion had finally attracted a half-dozen additional humans and Shades from the outside, who were shoving aside the shelves of cold cuts to flood in as backup.

"Plan F it is, then," Blot said.

Alan winced. "I really didn't like plan F," he said, kicking aside some of the shattered crate debris at his feet.

"That's why it wasn't plan A," Blot said, producing a second white cylinder with a dangling ring.

Alan didn't even pause to try to bluff them, he simply pulled the ring and gave the grenade a gentle toss to land at the feet of the approaching shifters.

"Do you *really* think we would fall for that twice?" scoffed one of the shifter's Shades.

"No. I really didn't," Alan said.

An acrid white smoke started pouring out of the grenade. Blot pulled Alan down into the shadows, and the pair nestled as tightly as they could into the overturned crate. An instant later, the flash-bang went off like a point-blank bolt of lightning. As shadows, Alan and Blot were spared the concussive blast of the grenade. Some of the light shone bright enough that it lanced through the cracks in the crate. It felt like he'd been lashed with a whip. Blot hissed in pain, but pulled them out and let him spring back to his feet.

The others had not been so lucky. Humans were stumbling or crawling. Shades were shuddering and twitching as if scalded with boiling water. Alan grabbed all but a dozen or so of the weapons scattered about his feet and sprinted for the open door to the mystically enhanced refrigerator. A few more members of the Shades crowded into the doorway. Alan was finally able to swing his camera around and snap a picture, staggering the shadows. Blot rose up out of the shadows, bulking herself into her combat form, but it was clear the rapid-fire use of her powers had drained her terribly, as she couldn't manage much more than an awkward shoulder tackle to knock the humans aside.

Alan skidded out onto the slippery, flooded floor of the sandwich shop that was still being doused by the sprinkler system. Chu-chu had outdone himself. The place was empty, with everyone who hadn't rushed into the refrigerator vault having evacuated, out of either fear or confusion. Thus, the rikt was perched on the shadow of the cash register, pecking at the lunch meat trays beside it.

"Chu-chu, I'm so proud! Let's go!" Blot shouted as Alan streaked past.

He stumbled onto the street, where eight additional Shade-afflicted humans were nursing the inevitable wounds from being in close quarters while such chaos was ensuing. The street was almost shoulder-to-shoulder with the lingering festivalgoers rubbernecking the madness.

Shouts of anger and violence were starting to spread, as the Shades in the street attempted to converge on Alan. The anger and fear turned out to be contagious, as a wave of hostility rushed through the crowd. But the way east was relatively clear. If Alan could get himself and Blot out of sight of the general public, and Blot could get Alan down into the shadows, they could surf the setting sun to the east, where Alan's car had been stashed for a quick getaway. Victory—or at least survival—was in sight.

A terrified squawk split the air, and Chu-chu burst from his perch. Bounding from shadow to shadow, dolphin-diving against the current of the sunlight, it fled west. Alan focused on pushing his way out of the donnybrook forming around him, ready to make his escape and fetch Chu-chu after. They could still make it.

"Stop," said a calm, commanding voice.

And she did. So did Alan. So did every last Shade and human on the street. Because the voice was not the voice of a human, it was the voice of a Glint.

A man and a woman with neutral expressions, pristine white suits, and white sunglasses stepped into view. They were Gabriel and Dina, the far less pleasant associates of Angel. Each carried a large silver briefcase.

"Well," Dina said. "It would appear our favorite agent has once again proved his worth."

"It would appear so," Gabriel said. "We really ought to make use of him more often."

"Ah, but his job has been so expertly done that it may no longer be necessary to do so," Dina said.

"Is that a promise?" Alan asked.

"Do not speak," Gabriel instructed. "Our discussions are so horribly tiresome. That you have served us well does not mean that you are good company. Reveal your spoils, would you?"

Alan dropped the sack of weapons he'd been clutching. Sacks and heaps of recovered Dawn goods lurched up from Blot's shadowy form as she obeyed the instructions. Dina picked up one of the daggers.

"So horribly coarse. Astounding they have so regularly held back the tide of the Shades with such things."

Gabriel plucked up a book and leafed through it. "They are not without their sages, however. I do believe this contains the information Angel requires for our little project."

He clicked open his briefcase and placed the book inside. Dina crouched down and eyed up the well-sealed boxes containing the Shards of Shadow. She opened her case.

"Mmm... contact with the Shades has had the anticipated effect. We may have what we need. I'll have those, thank you. Place them in the case so that we can prepare them for their ideal purpose," Dina said.

Alan couldn't help but obey, and Blot remained entirely inert as instructed, but he could feel her anger filtering up into his mind. Both Alan and Blot were unified in their desire to resist. More than anything else, the shards represented a possible end to this madness. In the hands of Gladys, they might actually give people the option to peacefully escape the clutches of their Shades in a way that would spare both the host *and* the Shade. And now, they were simply being taken away.

His muscles tensed. His jaw clenched. And he stopped himself a single step before reaching Dina. A single eyebrow arched above her sunglasses.

"Well. Disobedience. And I was just starting to like you."

She reached up and slid her glasses down her nose. Alan had no clear memory of the next few moments. One instant he was holding both boxes, steadfast in his desire to keep them from the Glints. The next his fingers were spread, his arms were trembling, and his vision was awash in blobs of purple and red, like he'd been staring at the sun. At the edge of his ailing vision, he saw Dina hefting the sealed briefcase in one hand and quickly slipping the other hand into the pocket of her suit. It was twisted and trembling as it slid from view, as though it had endured some terrible pain.

"That will be all," Gabriel said.

"As you were," Dina agreed. "The rest of you? Forget this."

The two marched through the front door of a building across the street. Slowly, each of the occupants of the street started to recover. To Alan's great concern, Blot and the Shades were recovering much more slowly than the humans. He blinked, trying to recover his vision, and dashed to the east.

"Blot! Blot, we need to get into the shadows. The car is a *long* way away."

"I'm... tired, Alan. The Glints... hit me hard..." she said.

111

He looked over his shoulder. His slowly recovering vision revealed that the other Shades seemed to be ailing as well. For the moment, it was a ridiculous foot race, with bewildered humans hosts who very likely had just experienced their first encounter with Glints. Or more accurately, they were grappling with a mysterious gap in their memory. But their minds were quickly clearing, and while Alan was fairly fit, at least a few of these humans were selected for their physical prowess and it showed. The only mercy was that the sun was still lingering in the sky, and the street was full of equally confused, non-Shade-bearing humans who did not take kindly to being shoved aside by those in pursuit of Alan. Like a chain reaction, each little cluster of humans angrily shoved back, scattering others into fresh clumps of confused and unhappy festivalgoers with bellies full of beer and crab. In moments, the street went from dizzied people trying to come to terms with a few seconds of missing memory to a full-scale brawl. Alan, for the sake of self-defense, spun a few times to snap pictures with unnecessary flashes to stagger the Shades.

Blaring sirens started to drown out the growing roar of the crowd as police and firefighters, responding to the still-screeching alarm, now found themselves tangling with a low-grade riot. The Shades wouldn't do anything supernatural in full view of them even when they recovered. But that just meant it was a race for the nearest dark alley.

Alan brandished his backup camera when the first camera's flash was depleted. He thumbed the standby button for the hefty flash.

"Blot," he said urgently, pulling his keys from his pocket. "It's now or never."

"I can do it, Alan. I can get it done."

He glanced over his shoulder. A large and very angry man with a larger and much angrier Shade was behind him, with the sun behind them both, which cast the Shade worryingly close to Alan's feet. He felt phantom claws reach up and slash at him, falling short, but just barely. Considering the spectacle of a firetruck was almost certainly drawing the attention of anyone within earshot, and that he'd probably die if he *didn't*, Alan was absolutely willing to risk a little broad-daylight Shade shenanigans.

He dove in desperation for the shadow of a mailbox. The moment it offered a moment of respite from the sun, Blot slid forward and didn't so much pull him into the shadows as catch him in the shadow. Once again held in silhouette, albeit barely, the pair slid out into the sun and surfed it along the street. Alan counted off the intersections as they went. Behind them, one of the humans ducked into an alley and darted back out, pulled into the shadows as well.

Blot wove to and fro, avoiding the slashing claws of the thing as the vicious Shade sought to drag Alan back out of the shadow. Finally they reached the right street, and Blot barely managed to ease them into the shaded cross street where Alan's car was waiting. She slid across the hood, through the windshield, and released him in the driver's seat, which he struck hard enough to force it to recline.

Scrambling to right himself, he jammed the keys into the ignition. Tires squealed and a figure sprang out of the shadows in front of him. A terrified swerve and an equally terrified dive barely prevented Alan from smearing the Shade's host across the pavement.

After a life of faithfully following every last traffic law, blowing through stop signs and traffic lights as he streaked across town felt like cutting off his own finger, but it was the lesser of two evils. He very much suspected if he didn't, then his fingers would be the least of the things he'd be losing.

Driving across town meant the Shades couldn't ride the sun to chase him, and soon there were none in his rearview mirror. They would no doubt be giving chase, but Blot and Alan had the stealth magic to make tracking them nearly impossible. They needed to head back to Philadelphia—perhaps not directly, since that would be a trifle obvious to those who might be after them.

"Make a right! Head west! Chu-chu'll head back to the stone. We have to get him!" Blot said.

Alan's fingers tightened around the steering wheel. "I can't believe I'm doing this," he said, making the turn. "We're running for our lives!"

"I don't want him to get lost," Blot said.

"He's never had a hard time finding us before."

"You saw him run when the Glint's showed up. What if he's still scared? He needs his mommy."

He drove toward the place they'd begun their little assault. Rather than stopping, he held his hand up out of the window as they drove past the soda machine. The sun cast Blot's shadow along the storefront, and when it passed where the stone had been stowed, she vanished it. As soon as they were back in the shadow of a row of buildings, Blot popped the rock back into reality.

"Did we do it?" Alan said, barely able to hear his own voice over the hammering of his heart in his ears.

Blot peered at the world outside, the tinted windows providing enough mobility for her to check all sides of the car.

"I don't see any Shades. I don't feel any nearby either. ... I think we did. I think we pulled this off."

"Good... Good... Let's never do this again..."

Chapter 7

Alan drove with the sort of stiff, twitchy reactiveness that only a supernatural near-death experience could inspire. It had taken less than two hours to get to Maryland. The route they'd chosen to take back was stretching to greater than four and they had yet to cross the city limits. Among the assorted bizarre results of this trip was a trunk filled nearly to overflowing with enchanted silver artifacts and magic writings, with at least that much or more still vanished by Blot. Alan also had a smoldering feeling in the back of his mind from having been both assaulted by the Glints and used as a reserve of strength for Blot's antics. Strangest of all, there was a full rack of raw pork ribs that were steadily disappearing into thin air as Chu-chu stripped them of their flesh and gulped down the bones.

"You know, I worried about what you were doing with all the coffee you drink, but this rikt has probably put away two-hundred pounds of treats since you adopted him."

"Don't worry about it. We have better things to worry about," Blot said, gazing out the window."

"Why, do you see something?" Alan said.

"Nothing. Still nothing," Blot said, scanning their surroundings. "I think we're in the clear in terms of pursuers."

"I don't think we're ever in the clear," Alan said.

"I'll tell you one thing about all this. No. I'll tell you *two* things about it. Three. I'll tell you *four* things about this," Blot said.

"You'd better get started or the list will keep growing," Alan said.

"First, I'm never vanishing a bag full of Dawn weapons again," Blot said. "I can feel them *poking* me, even through the bag. I feel bruised."

"You're taking one for the team. I'm glad you didn't get hurt. I can still feel that weird weakness from when you used some of my soul or whatever it is you use when you borrow power from me."

"You'll recover. Or would you rather I run out of pep right when we're surrounded by hostile Shades?"

"I'm glad you did what you did, but it's still unpleasant and unfamiliar. You were saying?"

"Right, right. Number one, no more vanishing Dawn gear. Number two, it still burns me that they took the shards."

"The Glints?"

"Did someone *else* come and take shards from us?" Blot snapped. "Those were *ours*."

"They were the Dawn's, I think."

"Right, but they stole them from *us*. The Shades, I mean."

"Did they?"

"Do you really think a bunch of *humans* made or found things that are the root and focus of Shade magic? Of *course* they stole them from us. I don't know when or how, but as far as I'm concerned, when the Shades took them, that was *right*. So keeping them would have been only proper. We keep them *away* from the Dawn *and* we keep them from the Shades who are probably going to use them in ways that'll cause problems. And then who comes along? The Glints. They're just about as far from a Shade as you can get. It's like Shades, then humans, *then* Glints. Which takes me to the third thing. I think they're afraid of us."

Alan raised his eyebrow. "Afraid of the Shades?"

"Think about it. They didn't need us to find that place. The Dawn knew basically where they were, and they're just as good at tracking people who are hidden with the magic the other Shades are using as we are, if not better. And they were *right there* when we got out. They could have walked right up to the door, said their little mumbly orders to make people listen, and had all those goods handed to them, no muss, no fuss. But did they? No. They made us do the dirty work. And they'll talk all day about how they don't get involved and balance this and balance that. But I think they're lying through their teeth. I think they don't want to tangle with the Shades because we have what it takes to hurt them."

"I'm not so sure."

"That's because somewhere in your head, you're still convinced they're angels."

"They're no angels," Alan said.

"Not in the 'perfect agents of goodness and virtue' sense, sure. Which, by the way, is nonsense. I've flipped through a couple different holy books since I came here, and angels are more fire and vengeance than goodness and light. But they're also *powerful*. And I've seen enough of your stress dreams to know that you see those Glints as invincible, insurmountable beings. And that's what they *want* you to believe. But I'm not fooled. They tried to wipe it out. Tried to wipe away the memory of it. But I saw that shaking claw of a hand Dina put in her pocket after she touched the *boxes* the shard was in. Just the *boxes*. And remember when Angel took one?

They used a big glove! And then they gave it back to us. Why? Because it's dangerous to them. And I think *we* are dangerous to them. What was that, three?"

"Yes."

"All right. And four is... four is... I don't remember what four was. Three is already enough. That's enough for—"

The phone chirped with a text message tone. Blot picked it up and glanced at it.

"It's Cox. He wants to know if we have any video footage."

"He should be thankful we took the time to load the pictures on the laptop and waste my mobile data sending them to him," Alan said. I'm sure he's just *delighted* at the 'on the ground' photos we had of the madness in the street."

"Oh, yeah. I forgot," Blot said, reaching into Alan's pocket to fetch Chu-chu's rock.

"Forgot what?"

"Chu-chu-chu," Blot trilled.

The rikt unwrapped itself from around the rock. Blot scratched it behind the neck, then pulled something away from the dark shadow of the creature. She released it, and a small black box popped into three dimensions. It was one of Alan's small collection of all-weather GoPros he'd picked up to experiment with.

"... You put a GoPro on Chu-chu?"

"Yep! I thought it might be interesting to see how that would go."

"Did any of it come out all right?" he said, stern disapproval pitifully failing to remain in place in the face of photojournalistic curiosity.

"Chu-chu!" she called sweetly. With some effort, she got it plugged in to a charger and navigated the little screen once it lit up. "It all looks a little off, but if we slice it up a little, I think we'll get some usable chunks. Should I reply with a bit as a teaser?" Blot said.

"Just let him know we might have something. Maybe it'll mean a little extra money in the bank if we survive it all."

Blot scrubbed the video she'd arranged for. In the madness, only a few relatively panicked shots ended up anything more than an oddly distorted blur, but Blot had enough of an eye for what Cox was after to know all it would take was five or six seconds of exciting footage and he'd be happy. She'd only just finished firing the message off when the phone rang again.

"It's Jessie," Blot said grumpily.

"Speaker phone," he said.

She tapped the appropriate button and dropped the phone on the seat.

"Alan?" Jessie said.

"Yeah. I'm almost back."

"Is that wacky stuff at the crab festival you?"

"I was in the middle of it for a bit."

"Did anyone get hurt?"

"Blot and I are a little sore, but I think things were fairly uneventful."

"According to the news, a sandwich shop was 'the scene of utter chaos amid a crab-based celebration.' Doesn't sound uneventful to me."

"Uneventful for us. Frankly, a little too smooth, considering the stakes for the Shades," Alan said.

"I was thinking that myself," Blot said.

"And you're sure you're not being followed?"

"As sure as I can be, which isn't very."

"I'm worried about you, Alan."

"That's just because you know what I've been doing. If you were more like my mom, who I have kept carefully in the dark about this stuff, you wouldn't have a care in the world."

"Your mom is still worried about you. She's a mom. She's just worried you're not getting enough vitamin C or you'll never find a nice girl."

"I guess. So what have you been up to?"

"Investigating a money laundering ring," Jessie said.

"Is that... is that really your department?" Alan asked.

"It is when it's being run by people with Shades. Do we have a name for that? It seems like it's the sort of thing that should have a less cumbersome name than 'people who have Shades.'"

"... You're investigating Shades?" Alan said.

"I'm the only one on the force who *can*. Thanks to Frightful."

"I don't think you should be risking interactions with Shades without me around. At least Blot and I are linked. Frightful could just fly off and leave you—"

"Exactly like everyone else. I'm a cop, Alan. I'm supposed to keep people safe. I'm supposed to enforce the law. And these people are breaking the law using Shade techniques. If this is the world we're living in now, then this is something that's going to have to be done, and I'm going to do it."

"You should be leaving stuff like that to me and Blot."

"You're not a cop. You're a contractor in the employ of the department. You don't have the authority to make arrests like this. Come to think of it, aren't you due to go on duty in a few hours."

"Yes..." he said wearily.

"You're serving a lot of masters right now, Alan. Leave this one to me. Frankly, if this works out, it might be worth trying to put together some sort of a 'Shade Enforcement Corps' within the force. I *may* have convinced one of the money launderers that there already was one. We just need to see if we can find more obliging rikts and/or more Shades like Blot who are willing to be a part of society rather than a part of a plot to overthrow it."

"If this whole thing lasts much longer, you're probably right. Something Blot and I have been working on *should* have made that more achievable, but the equipment we needed was claimed by someone who clearly thinks they are a higher authority."

"This is another situation where having an official branch of the police force for this sort of thing would have come in handy. No question about authority or jurisdiction."

"Yeah. I'm not sure these particular people would honor that power structure. Just... if you're going to be trying to arrest Shades, be careful."

"I'll be as careful as you are," she said.

"Ideally I'd want you to be more careful than that."

"Me too, but that's not the hand we've been dealt, is it?"

"One of these days I'm going to have to have a word with whoever's dealing these cards..." Alan grumbled. "So, what's the deal with the investigation?"

"The deal is I was able to get a Shade and human to confess in *precisely* the right way to justify a raid of the headquarters, and I've managed to arrange to be present for the raid."

"Are you sure this is a good idea?"

"It's what needs to be done. Whether or not it's a good idea is immaterial. It's all going down shortly."

"When?! Maybe I can get there in time to—"

"Police business, Alan. You'll be there *only* if they decide a photographer is needed and you're the one on duty."

"I... I guess there's nothing I can do to stop you."

"You guess right. I'll be fine, Alan. Me and Frightful are a well-oiled machine. I'll call you when it's over."

"You better."

"Talk to you then. Bye!"

"Bye. Good luck."

She hung up. Blot slipped the phone back in his pocket.

"So what do you think about this?" Alan asked.

Blot made a noncommittal sound and flipped a page on a stolen pad to scribble on it. Alan raised an eyebrow.

"Blot?" he said.

"You spend enough time talking to and about Jessie, don't expect me to contribute. She'll do what she's going to do. I'm just glad she finally broke you of the ridiculous policy of not talking on the phone while the car is in motion."

"Do you have a problem with Jessie? I thought you were getting along fine."

Blot counted out on her fingers. "She's got good taste in food. She takes good care of her rikt. That's two things that are worthwhile about her, which is two more things than most humans I have to deal with. But she's still a big problem looming on the horizon of my life, and I'm choosing to relish the time between then and now."

"I don't know what you—"

"Not talking about it. Maybe focus on the load of magic weaponry in your trunk and poking at me, which we still need to drop off, hmm?" Blot said.

Alan flared his nostrils and tightened his jaws. "This is going to get worse before it gets better, isn't it?" he grumbled.

"Bold of you to suggest it'll get better," Blot grumbled in turn.

Jessie, accompanied by three other officers, approached the door of the apartment building. It said something about how seriously the police department was taking the ATM thefts that they'd set up this raid for after midnight rather than wait another day. She tried to remain calm and keep her eyes open. Frightful had curled into her shadow, but seemed oddly tense, flexing her unseen talons in a way that caused Jessie's back to twitch with vague pins and needles. She hadn't shared the specific nature of the threat in this place with the other officers. They wouldn't have believed her, and there was no way for her to provide proof that wouldn't cause them to doubt their own sanity. In what was probably a for-the-best scenario, Frightful showed no interest in leaving her as a perch, and indeed held on far more firmly when other humans were around. It meant asking her to share her gift of being able to see Shades by giving the other officers a turn was likely out of the question, but it also meant the rikt wouldn't grab onto someone who wasn't ready to have the truth revealed.

In what was becoming an unpleasantly common experience, she'd carefully constructed a story that had only the faintest relationship with reality, but guided those around her into as near an approximation of the proper behavior as she could. So the other officers weren't prepared for mysterious, supernatural magic or unseen attackers from another world. But they were prepared for "possible attack animals" and "unregistered weapons." She'd run a thousand scenarios through her mind on how best to get the others to evacuate safely if they were headed into a situation they couldn't understand. Every few moments the nagging feeling of doubt, the feeling she may have gotten in over her head, urged her to pull the plug. She had no fewer than six different plans for preventing the bust from happening on short notice. But this was the world now. Her eyes had been opened. She could close them and pretend the Shades weren't real, but that wouldn't change things. This was important. This was how she would prove to herself that she could still navigate a world where Shades were a part of the law enforcement duty to society.

"Flashlights ready," she said quietly, opting to let one of the other officers take the lead at the door. "Informant said they keep things dark."

The others nodded and readied their big, chunky flashlights. The lead officer hammered the door.

"Philly PD. Open up!" he barked.

Jessie shivered a bit as she heard the distant, not-quite-natural sound of Shade voices mixing with human shouts.

"We *have* a warrant and we *will* enter," the officer shouted. "This is your last chance to cooperate."

She saw a darker form against the dark sidewalk slide out from beneath the door and whisk away. Then another. They were starting to escape. Her training said to pursue, but her training didn't allow for beings who could slip through any crack and move at incredible speed without a vehicle. Right now, the fewer Shades inside the better. There wasn't really much hope of making arrests. This was just sending a message, and hopefully disrupting the money laundering ring enough to force them to move on to some other scheme.

"We're coming in!" the lead officer shouted. He stepped back and drove his heel against the door, bashing the door open.

A flood of Shades that had no doubt drawn their hosts down into the darkness rushed out like a flock of bats. She tried to keep from flinching as they scattered around her. Powerful flashlights shined into the doorway. A handful of Shades were slammed against the far wall before scurrying away. Jessie and the others rushed inside.

The place was pitch-black inside, and it couldn't have been more clear that this place was being used as the nerve center of some criminal enterprise. They'd done everything short of knocking down walls and installing heavy machinery in their quest to make this building a streamlined warehouse for the execution of their money laundering scheme. The doors had been removed from each of the apartments. Money had been scattered about, spilled upon the floor like litter. There wasn't nearly enough of it to account for the size of the operation she knew they were running. The way what remained was haphazardly thrown to the floor suggested they'd made a mad grab to collect as much of it as they could when the cops had arrived.

"Someone must've tipped them off," suggested the lead officer. "The place is deserted."

"Plenty of evidence left behind, though," Jessie said, nudging the bills with the toe of her boot. "We should head downstairs. According to the informant, the records were kept down there."

"Go. I'll keep an eye on things up here," he said.

She nodded and made her way toward the stairs at the far side of the hallway. Frightful was getting progressively more fidgety as she approached the steps. It wasn't fear. At least, it didn't feel like it. If anything, it felt like the rikt was getting excited about something. Like there was a feeling of anticipation.

Jessie crept down the stairs with one of the other officers into what had clearly once been the laundry room of the building. There was something grimly ironic about it becoming the center of a money laundering ring. Again, the place was free of humans and Shades as far as she could tell, but the place was a jackpot when it came to evidence. Unlike the piles of cash that must have been around until a few seconds before they kicked the door open, the incriminating information was almost entirely intact. Bulletin boards that probably once held flyers for open mics at comedy clubs or local bands trying to find gigs were now pinned with addresses and schedules that were a precise match for the ATMs and the timing of their restocking.

"This is it. This is the smoking gun," said the other officer. "These idiots took the money, but left us everything we need to lock them up for good."

"Yeah," Jessie said. "Almost like they think it won't matter. Like they think we'll never be able to catch them to lock them up."

"They've got another thing coming if they think that."

She swept her flashlight about.

"What are you looking for?" he asked. "We have everything we need right here."

She squinted and swept the room again. "This room only has one door, and no windows," she said.

"... So?"

"A room this size, a structure this size, needs at least two. Fire code," she said.

"I think that particular violation is the least of their concerns."

"Yeah," she said. "Still."

She tried to conjure to mind the general layout of the building. The south-facing emergency exit of the building would be not far past the west wall of this room. That meant there should be an emergency exit in or near this room on the west wall that led to the outside.

Jessie pulled her radio from her belt. "Do we have anyone near the alley on the south side of the building?" she said.

"Yeah. What's up? Do we have a runner?" came a swift reply.

"Can you give me the status of the emergency exit?" she said, marching out into the darkened hallway.

There was no emergency exit marker, but there was the bent remains of two mounting bolts. They'd possibly removed the sign in an attempt to render the place utterly dark. Perhaps there was another reason, but she couldn't figure out what it might be.

"Uh... Looks like there's a Dumpster shoved up against it," came the reply.

She found a snack machine awkwardly positioned in the hallway and leaned aside to shine the flashlight behind it. The door for the stairwell was hidden behind it. Not only was it hopelessly blocked, she could see that the door was chained.

"Anyone up there on the entry floor, check for a fire exit and stairwell on the south wall please? The markers may have been removed and the doors may have been blocked."

"We're a little busy collecting evidence," barked someone down the stairs rather than answering via the radio.

She gritted her teeth and walked back into the laundry room, now certain there was another exit to the room hidden somewhere. Two metal restaurant-style shelving units were shoved against the west wall, and a broken bracket on the ceiling marked where the exit sign had been mounted. Behind them, brown paper had been taped to the wall. The shelves were on wheels, easily rolled aside. She tugged at the peeling painter's tape holding the paper in place and revealed another exit to the stairwell. This one was chained as well.

"Can I get a call on this? Does our warrant cover breaking these chains to investigate the evacuation stairwell?" she said over the radio.

"Absolutely," came the reply.

"Then I'm going to need some bolt cutters," she said.

While other officers entered the laundry room to help catalog the evidence, an emergency crew provided the requested tools. She snipped the lock and carefully tested the door. She almost jumped out of her skin when Frightful shifted, peering up with interest. She muscled the door open and braced herself for what it might hide.

The answer turned out to be... nothing. It was just a stairwell. Every single entrance or exit from the stairwell was blocked, generally from the other side. But there was no cash hidden anywhere. No further incriminating evidence. Nothing but a utility hatch, which was also heavily chained but revealed little more than some plumbing and electrical conduits when opened.

"Why would they go out of their way to lock this place up?" Jessie mused.

"Probably didn't want any rival gangs or anything coming in to steal their cash," said one of the other cops.

She gazed at the open utility hatch, then at the white eye of the rikt where it was cast on the wall by her fellow officer's flashlight.

"Yeah," she said doubtfully. "That must be it…"

Several hours later, Blot and Alan were back in town and back off the clock. Despite starting his shift at the station as their forensic photographer not long after Jessie had gone out on her bust, the crime scene was far too straightforward for him to be deployed, so he'd spent most of his time in the station dozing off while waiting for a dispatch call that never came. They'd let him go a little early, though he was still on call for a few more hours.

He should have gone home. He and Blot had taken great pains to ensure that their home was safe, after all. But Blot had convinced him to delay returning there. Her reasoning, and presently he couldn't find much fault in the logic, was that the safety of their home had been provided via a Glint enchantment. And right now their opinion of the white-suits was at an all-time low. So instead, they'd decided to head to the all-night diner for some halfway-decent coffee, a stable Wi-Fi connection, and a hearty meal.

"I hope they tinker with those shards and melt their faces off," Blot said.

"It's a good thing they can't hear you," Alan said, tapping at his laptop, which was balanced on the table beside a Caesar salad he was working on.

"I wish they could. *And* I wish they could understand my native language. Because no offense to you and your kind, but us Shades have got some proper profanities. Things that'd curl your hair."

"I'm told the French have good curses."

"I speak French. They have *pretty* curses. And I don't know about you, but I'm not after *pretty* when I'm speaking that particular part of my mind. That older language I speak has some good ones, though. Things appropriate to thieves who would steal stuff that we stole back from people who stole them back from people who stole them in the first place."

"... What?" Alan said.

"Never mind. *She's* here," Blot said.

Alan looked up to see Jessie, in the not-quite-fully-applied uniform that suggested she was off duty but straight from the station.

"There she is! The woman of the hour," Alan said, closing his laptop and sliding aside to give her room to sit in the booth.

"Let me tell you something. If you don't like paperwork, don't go out on a bust like that. Four hours of collecting evidence, then four more of cataloging it. I hate racking up overtime with pencil-pushing."

"Still, you did something incredible, even if most people will never know *how* incredible," Alan said.

She flopped down and sighed. "I'm not sure how much good it'll do," she said quietly. "We both know we're never going to be able to find or hold any of the people who ran. What we've done here is create a bunch of fugitives. Tons of fingerprints in the system are now associated with at-large money launderers. Best case, we convinced the Shades to move their operations somewhere else. But at least they know they're not untouchable. What about you?"

"I raided a compound, stole back most of a pseudo-cult's gear, which is weighing down my trunk and giving Blot indigestion, and now I'm waiting to get a drop-off point from them so I can restore the effective stalemate between them and Blot's people. Hardly feels like an unalloyed victory."

"You know what? I think a technical victory is the best sort of victory we can hope for right now, so I say we use this excuse to celebrate. What do you think, Blot?"

Blot grumbled under her breath.

"Something wrong?" Jessie asked.

"She's particularly sore about some precious parts of the heist that we didn't get to hold on to," he said.

"Hey *hey*!" called the waitress, trotting over to the booth. "If it isn't my *two* favorite regulars."

Alan and Jessie turned and smiled. There were few things more wholesomely delightful than having someone at a neighborhood hangout remember you. And this waitress— "Honey" if her name tag could be believed—had precisely the sort of unpredictable hours to align with Alan's and Jessie's similarly unpredictable visits to the restaurant.

"Boy oh boy," she said, presenting a menu to Jessie. "The news has been wacky today, hasn't it?"

"I don't watch the news much these days," Alan said. "It's a little too close to my various day jobs."

"Yeah, yeah. I get that. Gotta have hobbies. That'll keep you sane. Provided your hobbies are sane, that is."

"Have you got any hobby recommendations?" Jessie said. "I feel like these days I could use a little extra sanity insurance."

"You could do what I did," she said, rummaging around in her apron. "Join a club."

"Oh yeah?" Alan said. "Which club?"

"Oh, it's a small one, but you may have heard of it."

She pulled a strange gadget from her apron and placed it on the table. It looked like a gyroscope or top, except it was attached to its base. She gave it a spin and it hissed along, well-oiled and perfectly balanced such that it seemed like it wasn't even slowing down. Once she was certain it was merrily on its way, she took a seat beside Jessie.

"It's called the Dusk," she said with a twinkle in her eye.

CHAPTER 8

In a tumultuous time in a person's life, the most precious thing that one can have is a safe place. Not just a place free from danger, but a place of comfort, and of freedom from the sources of that tumult. It might be a real place, a warm, secure home filled with loved ones. It could be something more abstract, a precious moment to escape into fiction, or to throw one's mind fully into the enjoyment of a sport. For Alan, Blot, and Jessie, there was the subtle but very real feeling that this diner, with its dimly lit booths and bottomless cups of coffee, was as near to a sanctuary as they would have. To have the waitress, the woman who moments before was only expected to provide some playful banter and supply Jessie with her beloved "breakfast for dinner," suddenly say the name of a secret society that even the *other* secret society didn't seem to know about felt like a horrible breach of the social contract.

"I... Did you..." Alan stuttered.

"Don't. Say. *Anything*," Blot instructed.

"Let me save you some time," Honey said, picking up Alan's coffee cup and mopping underneath it out of habit. "You are Alan Fontaine, you are Jessie Hearst, and somewhere over there is a brave and increasingly infamous Shade called Blot, who I can't see. Shades are shadow creatures that are visible only to humans with Shades or, as has recently been discovered, humans with excellent relationships with rikts, like Jessie's partnership with..." She snapped her fingers. "Fearful?" she said.

"F-frightful..." Jessie said.

"So close," Honey said. "You are fresh off a trip to steal back the equipment used by a group called the Dawn who, despite being devoted to eliminating Shades even at the cost of their hosts, is in an active partnership and/or truce with Alan and Blot. You were successful in acquiring most, if not all, of the gear, but one or more beings who have identified themselves to you as Glints stole some of the items, most notably one or more Shards of Shadow. That about cover it?"

"I... Yeah, that's about right," Alan said.

"She said I'm infamous..." Blot said with equal parts wariness and giddiness.

"Is it safe for you to know all that?" Jessie said.

"No! Fortunately, I have this thing here," she said, pointing to the gadget still spinning on the table. "They told me I should tell you about how it works, because otherwise it'd be difficult to get you to speak candidly. This is a... they have this whole big name for it. It's like... celestial reminiscence resonator or something ridiculous like that. I just call it the doohickey. It's the only way the Dusk has found to keep things hidden from the Glints outside of hiding them in some kind of shady spots that they also had a big fancy name for that I forgot. And it's *very* difficult to find a situation where one will work. Basically you need to have a place where the specific people in a conversation have had other conversations that weren't of interest to the Glints, then get those people together in that place and give the doohickey a spin, and it will sort of replay one of the uninteresting ones for the Glints if they're looking in the direction. Now's when you're supposed to test that."

It took Alan a few seconds to realize he was in a position to have to respond. "I... don't think we really need to test it, because this many mentions of the Glints and this much revelation would have for sure made them show up, since I'm pretty sure the way we found to hide from them doesn't cover you or Jessie."

"Good. Forgive me for talking fast. They told me the doohickey's effects only last as long as one of the past conversations, and we don't kibitz nearly long enough for me to cover everything without leaving and coming back. Plus, I have other tables to serve. So that sets the stage, don't talk freely unless this thing is spinning. It'll start slowing down when it's time to give it a rest. Got it?"

Alan blinked. "Yeah."

"Great!" She snatched the "doohickey" and dropped it into her apron. "So what can I get you, Officer?"

"... Pancakes with blueberries and whipped cream and a glass of skim milk," Jessie said, forcing herself to be steady. "And a side of bacon. Underdone if you can manage it."

"The piggie will still be squealing. I'll have that back for you in a minute and we'll do a little more chitchat."

She walked away as though she *hadn't* just revealed herself to be an agent of an arcane order.

"What just happened, Alan?" Blot said.

Alan took a moment to gather his thoughts and find a way to articulate them in an innocuous way. "You know something," he said in what he hoped was a convincingly conversational way. "I was talking to someone a while back about how sometimes you need help a little closer to you. An older woman. A gardener. I forget her name. Anyway, she said you never know when someone you didn't realize you knew will reveal himself or herself to be an old friend."

"Oh... Right, right. I remember now. Gladys said we'd met a member of the Dusk already. It was the *waitress*? I didn't see that coming."

"I wish she'd brought me a glass of ice water," Jessie said. "My mouth has suddenly gone dry..."

After a few more brief appearances, Honey provided Alan's main course—a chicken-fried steak—and Jessie's meal. She set the doohickey on the table and gave it a spin again.

"Right, so. Are we all settled? Ready for the real conversation," Honey asked.

"I get the feeling we're not going to have time for *nearly* the number of questions I have in mind," Alan said. "So let's just get started."

She clapped. "Great. We'll start with the big stuff. How many shards were there?"

"Two," Alan said. "I think, at least. There were two boxes. I think there were supposed to be three, but we only found two."

"The Dusk wants them. They can do good stuff with them, apparently. They didn't tell me much, but I believe them. And, more importantly, the Dusk wants to make double-sure that the Glints don't have them."

"Why?" Jessie said.

Honey shrugged. "Apparently they can do some serious damage with a 'fully-charged' shard? It must be bad, because what they're recommending is you steal them back from the Glints."

"That's not possible," Alan said. "They're incredibly powerful and basically all-seeing."

"Not so. Powerful, yes, but not nearly all-seeing. Apparently there are *very* few of them actively working on things like this. Names... Dina, Gabriel and... there's another one."

"Angel," Alan said.

"Right. Those three are *basically* the only ones paying any attention to the whole East Coast. They are stretched *thin*. And while they can certainly see mostly what they *choose* to see, they can only see one thing at a time. Apparently they'd be hard-pressed to observe even this entire restaurant with any reasonable level of detail. So you get all of them watching the same thing and every *other* thing in the area is no longer being watched, you dig?"

"That makes sense," Jessie said.

"So all you need is something that'll catch their undivided attention. Emphasis on undivided. Apparently the first two are mostly keeping their eyes on big groups of Shades doing battle or hatching schemes, and Angel is mostly just watching *you*. So if you want them to be completely focused on one place, you need something that'll have a big fight *and* you in one place, Alan."

"We just missed our chance," Alan said. "That whole fiasco in Maryland."

"You're overlooking just what's liable to happen when you hand over the equipment to the Dawn."

"Right," Blot said. "Either the Shades will try to stop the handover, or the handover will happen and the Dawn will try to move on the Shades."

"Is she talking?" Honey asked, pointing at not quite the right place to indicate Blot. "I don't want to interrupt."

"How did you know she was talking at all?"

"You looked distracted."

"Well, she is picking up what you're laying down," Alan said. "But there's still the issue of how to actually *steal* from the Glints. It's not as though *we'll* be able to do it. Like you said, Angel will be watching us."

"Right, right. It has to be someone in the loop who they aren't actively watching. *That's* the person who can sneak in and get the shards."

"Are you suggesting *you* could do it?"

Honey scoffed. "No! No, no, no. There may not be a lot of Glints working, but there's even fewer members of the Dusk. The fact they recruited a waitress gives you an idea of how desperate they are for new blood. No, the Dusk is thinking more along the lines of Jessie."

"What? Me?" Jessie said.

"You *are* here celebrating with pancakes after thwarting the forces of evil," Honey said.

"It's one thing to use the partnership with Frightful to chase away some money launderers. It's another to *rob a group of supernatural entities.*"

"We did it a little. I stole some silver," Blot said. "It didn't go so bad. They made me forget about it, but I eventually remembered. They can't do much if they're not there. Just go and steal."

"I will use the resources available to operate *within* the law to *uphold* the law," Jessie said. "I won't use them to *break* the law."

139

Honey shrugged. "They recruited me to let you know what's what, not to persuade you to do things. You can keep the doohickey, I have another. Take it out in a place where you and the person you're planning to talk to have had conversations that you didn't need to hide and give it a spin. If it keeps spinning, you know you're good until it stops. Also, they told me to give you this." She placed a fat, folded stack of pages on the table. "Read the whole thing. Apparently it's very detailed. Enjoy your meal. I'll be back to check if you need a refill."

The group remained silent for a few moments. Blot was the first to speak.

"I wouldn't have believed her, except she seems to know a lot about us," Blot said. "And I wouldn't have trusted her, except she's the only harbinger of news and wisdom that *also* brings me coffee."

Alan leaned his face on his hands. "I feel suddenly much less safe here... Let's finish up and head to my place. We have a lot more to discuss."

A short, silent ride home in two separate cars brought them to Alan's apartment. Despite everything, it was intact. For all of the things the Glints had been doing, their enchantment upon the apartment had kept it free of attack even though the Shades absolutely knew who lived there and what he had done. It took a few sweaty trips to haul the several hundred pounds of Dawn gear into the apartment and hide it in every available bit of space, but once they were through, they could take a moment to address all that had happened, and all they had learned.

Alan and Jessie took a seat on the couch. Blot set Chu-chu's special rock on an adorable little velvet pillow in the drawer of the side table. When all was ready, Blot produced the doohickey and set it on the table, giving it a spin. She grinned.

"Can you feel it? I can," Blot said. "It's like a gentle cool breeze in the back of my mind. This is *wonderful*. I love this thing. I wonder if I can figure out how they made it."

"Later," Alan said. "If we're only going to be able to have little chunks of being safe from view, we need to spend them well. First up, the pages."

Blot twiddled her fingers, producing the packet Honey had given them. "Good thinking. Start with the stuff they're trying to teach us, *then* move on to what we can find out on our own. Let's see what we have." She flipped through the pages, speaking with the rushed tone of someone reading something from a page that they are impatient to be through with. "The Glints are not capable of directly perceiving Shades, and as far as we know they cannot be made capable of doing so under any circumstances. They are, however, capable of detecting the presence of Shades who are paired with humans. Any regression into a Shade-specific mode of existence or environment will completely remove a Glint's capacity to oversee one's direct actions. As such, unless they have chosen to assert themselves physically, Shades can speak freely without fear of being overheard. Areas supernaturally distorted or created by Shades are similarly imperceptible. Though magic capable of extending this imperceptibility to non-Shades is not difficult to formulate, like a stone dropped into the surface of a pond, it is difficult to vanish from sight without the evidence of one's disappearance remaining visible."

She looked up from the page. "Why does it always end up with metaphor?" she said.

Alan glared at the spinning doohickey, as if by doing so he could will it to continue spinning. "Keep going," he said.

"Uh... It repeats what Honey said about how they aren't omniscient, and how they're stretched thin, so they can only watch a few things at a time. Oh! It says here you should make a habit of wearing silver jewelry. It's always silver, I wonder why that is."

"Why silver jewelry, Blot?" Alan asked.

"I'm getting to it." She murmured under her breath. "Here it is. Relatively pure silver becomes detectably warmer when one is under direct observation by a Glint, if first the following enchantment is applied." Her white eyes narrowed. "The enchantment seems easy enough. It says here the enchantment is a weak 'wedge' in the power of the Glints. It makes people aware of their 'glamour' and thus facilitates resistance to it."

"Does that mean they won't be able to issue orders to us when we are wearing enchanted silver?" Alan said hopefully.

"I'm reading..." Blot said. "No, no. 'The Glint power of compulsion is intrinsic and cannot be circumvented through any enchantment known to us.'"

"Then what's that glamour thing?"

"It means, like... if they're using their power to convince you of something that isn't true. Illusions and stuff." She scanned more of the document. "And only if you are able to physically contact them with the enchanted jewelry itself. Not a particularly strong enchantment. But a whole lot better than nothing."

"Shame I'm not much for jewelry," Jessie said.

"We have the Dawn stuff, but it's mostly pendants and knives. Not the kind of stuff you could keep on you," Alan said. "Blot can enchant that beat-up Dawn pendant we were using to test the stealth enchantment and just pay attention to it for both of us."

"Maybe I can head to a pawn shop and find something cheap," Jessie mused.

"Wait... Just a minute. I might have something. Talk loud, Blot. What else does it say?" Alan thumped off to his bedroom and started opening and shutting drawers.

"There's really not much more. They make it *very* clear we can't expect any sort of help that might expose the Dusk more than they've already been exposed. Their role is mostly hiding and trying to figure out how to solve problems with limited resources. There's a bit here about something they've been tinkering with that could 'more fully and actively pierce the Glint veil' in their words."

"What's that mean?" Jessie said.

"The Glints can hide things," Blot said. "I guess the Dusk thinks they might be able to actively reveal them. They have instructions here for how to see through Glint glamours. They say if you think something was taken from your memory, you might be able to restore it if you look for the gaps they've created rather than the things that should be in the gaps. But the Dusk is still trying to find a way to actually wipe away that 'glamour.' Why is it when Shades do stuff, it's words like 'stained' or 'twisted' or 'distorted'? But when the Glints do stuff, it's 'glamour'? Why do the Glints get words associated with fashion models and we get words associated with mold?"

"Here! Found it," Alan said, marching out of the room with a dingy, yellowed envelope. "This is my grandmother's ring. She left it to me when she passed. I'm pretty sure it's high-quality silver."

"Will it fit you? Maybe then you can give me the Dawn pendant and I can keep it in my pocket or something," Jessie said.

"What? No, this is for you." Alan held it out for Blot to inspect. "Is it enough for the enchantment?"

"It'll do, I think," Blot said. "Let me give it a try on this first. It doesn't already have a Dawn enchantment, so it should be easier to apply the Dusk magic to it."

The ring vanished into the shadows. For a few moments, Blot glanced back and forth between the pages from the Dusk and the silhouette of the ring.

"You're giving me your grandmother's ring?" Jessie said.

"It's that or leave it in an envelope. Besides, Grandma left it to me 'in case I ever meet a nice girl.'"

Blot released a semidisgusted sound, but continued working at the ring. "I'm going to need some more of your oomph."

"Whatever it takes," Alan replied.

He felt the supernatural tug once more. Like so many things in his life, it was a withering, unpleasant sensation that was becoming uncomfortably familiar to him.

"And we're sure all this will work?" Jessie said. "I know I'm in an apartment with a talking shadow and two shadow birds, but I'm still not quite on board with the idea of magic."

"Well, get used to it," Blot said. "Because if Dusk magic is all as easy as this, I'm going to be trying to learn a lot more of it."

She produced the ring and handed it to Alan, who immediately handed it over to Jessie.

"I think I did it right," Blot said. "I felt something sort of... slide into place and stay there. Which is mostly how the other enchantments have felt when I got them right."

"I'm touched," Jessie said, taking the ring.

"It'd feel like a much more touching gesture to me if it wasn't to warn you about supernatural surveillance that you probably wouldn't have to worry about if not for me," said Alan.

"It's still very sweet," Jessie said, testing the ring until she found a finger it fit. "This is good, isn't it. If it really does work, this'll solve a lot of things. I'll have a way to know if I'm being watched, and we know that everything *Blot* says is secret. So as long as I'm not being watched, Blot can pull your phone into the shadow and call me and we can have a proper discussion, and the only one who can't speak freely is *you*. Which I guess means Blot and I will be having a lot more conversation just between the two of us."

"Lovely," Blot said with a bit less enthusiasm.

"I'm not terribly pleased with how involved you're having to get, Jessie," Alan said.

"I'm not terribly pleased with it either," Jessie said.

"Neither am I," Blot said quickly. "So this is something we all agree about."

"Still. It isn't like this is the only thing in my life I wish I didn't have to deal with. And it's good that we *have* a way to deal with it. Or at least to make plans," Jessie said.

"But the question is, what sort of plans are we going to make?" Alan said. "Are you going to do what they want you to do? Are you going to try to infiltrate the Glints and get the Shards of Shadow back?"

Jessie ran her fingers through her hair. "Setting aside that I'm not sure how we'd do it, I just don't think I can justify it. We don't even know what they intend to use them for or if their intentions are bad."

"They're not going to be *good*," Blot snapped.

"But it's still possible that what the Glints want to do is better than what the Shades or the Dawn wanted to do. Say what you will about the Glints, they don't seem to have been doing very much directly. So if the Shards of Shadow just get tucked away somewhere, that's probably for the best."

"Disagree," Blot grumbled.

"Can we agree that regardless of everything else, we should find a way to defuse what's sure to be a *very* bloody clash between the Shades and the Dawn?" Alan said.

"Absolutely," Jessie said. "There's a huge capacity for people to be badly hurt or killed."

"... I suppose..." Blot said. "I don't have much love for the Dawn, but the only way we're going to get through this without one side annihilating the other is going to be if we can keep the blood off the claws of my kind long enough to convince *your* kind that we're not wholly and exclusively dedicated to getting our claws bloody."

"So if that's what we're in agreement on, then we'll work on that. So let's get down to it," Alan said.

Several hours of brainstorming had failed to produce much meaningful progress. A clash between two forces that had been shaped by one another for the precise purpose of wiping each other out seemed either inevitable or an act of suicide to attempt to stop. Jessie had taken to scribbling down ideas and reading over them as though if she scrutinized every letter, some revolutionary new technique would come tumbling out of the page.

"What about—"

"Shh!" Blot hissed.

Jessie glanced aside at the doohickey. "It's still spinning," she said. "What's... Oh..."

When she looked up, she found that Alan had slumped back in the chair, exhaustion finally having claimed him.

"Where's he keep his spare blankets?" she said quietly.

"It's fine. I'll tuck him in. You can just leave," Blot said.

"It's really no trouble," Jessie said.

"Leave, Jessie," Blot said steadily.

Jessie tipped her head. "Blot, do we have a problem? Because if we do, we should talk about it."

"Not this," Blot said in frustration. "It's bad enough you talked him into going to that nosy therapist who just picks and pokes and tries to get him to 'embrace' or 'address' or whatever else she thinks it'll take to get rid of me. I don't need *you* doing the same."

"Blot, this is your home as much as his. If you need me to go, I'll go. But right now we are in something very dangerous, and we're going to need each other to get through it."

"We were getting along just fine without you. The only reason I stepped up and revealed myself to you was because I didn't want him to blame me for pushing you away. But don't get me wrong. I don't need you. And we both know if it comes down to it, and if it is remotely possible, he's going to choose you over me."

"This isn't a 'you or me' situation, Blot."

"He's smitten with you. All right? He seems to teeter back and forth on being able to accept that, but *you're* at least sharp enough to know it."

"We're just friends," she said.

"Maybe you believe that. And maybe he says that to himself. But trust me, if he heard you *say* that, he'd be devastated. By the void, he just gave you his grandmother's ring. I'm from another *world* and I see the symbolism."

"Even if all this is true, why would that be cause for all this coldness?"

"Because he's your friend, or mate, or whatever you two are going to decide he is to you. But he's my *world*."

"I can't force you out, and I wouldn't even if I could. You know he's going to do right by you. And if we're lucky, he'll find a way to get his shadow back and you'll be able to find a host who—"

"What if I don't *want* to leave? Hmm? What if, *despite* all the danger, this little partnership, which is just an *affliction* for him, is the best thing that ever happened to me? I'm getting stronger. I'm learning. I have a person I can trust. We work well together. I have *Chu-chu*. I don't just need Alan. I want him. I don't *want* another host. He's not the kind of human I've been taught to seek out, and I think I know why. First, because we'd never be able to find enough people like him even if we'd been trained to find them. He's pretty much one of a kind. And second, if we *did* find hosts like him, we'd lose the will to take over this world, because we'd be happy just being a *part* of it."

Blot glanced at Alan to be sure he was still asleep. When he released a grating snore, she turned back to Jessie. "He's my world," she repeated. "And the closer you get, the smaller my world gets. Not because you take away from him, but because you take him away from *me*. There's only so much Alan to go around. And I'm not so selfish as to push you away when you're the person he wants. He deserves to have the life he wanted for himself. He didn't have to be nice to me. But don't expect me to be happy about it as I get shoved over to the wall while you share the bed."

Blot cast herself along the floor, then up onto the table in lieu of leaning closer to Jessie. "You're even in his *dreams...*" she rumbled.

"Blot, I don't know how to assure you that things will be fine between us. I guess there's no way to be sure that they *will* be. But for now, until this madness is over, we're going to have to make it work."

"I know. I know. And that's the thing. The madness might never end. For all we know, right now the very thing we've been trying to puzzle out how to prevent is happening. It isn't as though we have any *real* insight into what the Shades are thinking. In the name of darkness, Alan and I didn't even know about that money laundering ring you found. I almost wish you hadn't broken it up. Maybe we could have gotten a hold of one of the Shades and I could have tried to get a little more out of them than you did."

Jessie looked up, realization dawning. "Wait... We *do* have members of the Shades available to us," she said. "Active members of the Shades. There's the one we got a confession out of, but there's also Todd."

"The shape shifter?" Blot said. "How are you going to get anything out of *him*? How are you going to *find* him?"

"He's still in prison," she said.

149

"No... Seriously?"

"Yes! After the zoo incident, he was arrested, and he didn't even bother to defend himself. He ended up getting shifted over into what's become of the cellblock that you and Alan locked down with Brink."

"Why in this world is he still there? He could easily tear the door off his cell or just pull into the shadows and slide underneath them."

"Beats me. But I know he's still in there because I know the guy who does the prisoner transfers and he thinks Todd is the funniest thing he's ever seen. Apparently he's never stopped acting drunk despite being in a prison where alcohol is unavailable. I've got to imagine he's still one of the more powerful physical specimens the Shades have, so they're *bound* to want him to be a part of the clash. I can't believe I didn't think of this before."

"Will you be able to talk to him?" Blot said. "I don't think it's wise for Alan and I to try to. It would probably cause a scene, and the prison made it pretty clear they didn't want any part of us coming back inside after our photos caused them such a black eye in the press."

"I think I can manage it. I'll try it as soon as I can. Sometime tomorrow." She checked her watch. "I should go. There's lots to do," she said, standing.

She turned to the door, then turned back. "... He dreams of me?"

"He's doing it right now." Blot shut her eyes. "The two of you are sitting around a campfire. You're putting together some sort of dessert cooked over the fire." The corner of Blot's mouth teased at a grin. "I'm there too. Not this me. The real me. The one that's not a shadow. I'm critiquing your technique in assembling the... s'mores?"

"Seems like he's making space for you even in his dreams," Jessie said.

Blot opened her eyes. "For a brief and dim moment before you got close, he didn't have to make room for me. I was just there. It was taken for *granted* I'd be there."

"Blot, I'll ask this, and you don't even have to answer if you don't want to. I'm asking it for you more than I'm asking for me. When you think about losing him, and losing space in his mind, does that hurt you because you're afraid you'll matter less to him and your life will be harder to manage with me in it? Or are you hurt because you wish he felt for you the way you believe he feels for me?"

Blot glared at her from the table for a long, tense moment. "I think that's enough for today, Jessie," she said steadily. "Talk to Todd. Tell us what you learn."

"I will. And we're going to figure this out, Blot. One way or another, we're going to figure this out."

Chapter 9

Alan wearily dragged himself from bed and blinked at the clock. As the foggy mists of sleep started to part, he realized it was nearly eleven a.m. Once enough of his brain's logic had kicked in, reality hit him like a hammer to the back of the skull.

"I missed the scrum!" Alan yelped, tumbling out of bed and fumbling for clothes in the near total darkness his blackout curtains provided.

"Check your phone," Blot shouted from the other room.

She, as was often the case in the mornings, had stretched herself to the kitchen to tinker with whatever she'd decided the morning culinary experiment would be. Alan fumbled for his phone and found a lengthy text message exchange between Mr. Cox and, apparently, himself. It had become somewhat heated, but had concluded with the agreement to provide the six useful clips of the footage from Chu-chu's rampage in lieu of taking a new assignment for the day.

"You got nearly twice the going rate," Alan said. "*And* a day off?"

"You should let me do your negotiating more often," Blot said.

"But why did you *do* that?" Alan said.

"Because you've had *maybe* three hours of sleep in the past two days, and you weren't exactly all caught up on your sleep before that either. You're still not recovered from the strength I had to borrow from you to pull off the heist from the other Shades and do *two* enchantments. Sooner or later we're going to face some pushback from *someone*, and you're not going to be any good to us if you're dozing off."

He checked his phone again. There was also a text from Jessie letting him know she'd gotten home okay. "I don't suppose you two came up with a good plan for what to do next while I was sleeping," he said.

"We didn't do much planning once you passed out." Blot lowered her voice. "She's a little too insightful for her own good sometimes..."

"What's *that* supposed to mean?" he said.

"Nothing. Breakfast is done. Or brunch, I guess. Come and get it."

He started to get changed, pausing briefly. "I don't remember going to bed."

"You didn't. You passed out in the chair," she said.

"I also don't remember getting undressed."

"You didn't."

"So how, may I ask, did I end up in bed and in my pajamas?"

"You know how I can pull you into the shadows?" she said.

"Yeah?"

"I don't *have* to bring your clothes with you. The tricky part was laying out your pajamas in such a way that I could pop you back up into them."

"But I... But you..." Alan tried to pick which of the many things about that were worth objecting to. "I need to hold my breath when I'm in the shadows. How'd you do that while I was asleep?"

"You don't *really* need to hold your breath. You just *think* you do, and what you think about what you do matters a lot more when you're in the shadows, because you're more thought than anything else. So while it's true that if you could convince yourself you didn't have to breathe, we'd be able to stay in the shadows a lot longer. But since you *can't* convince yourself you don't have to breathe, you really *will* suffer the consequences if you don't do it."

"So being a Shade is like... having all of reality be a placebo?"

"Let's just say we have our own rules we have to follow, and the ones you have to follow are more flexible."

"Well, regardless. I appreciate it, but next time, wake me up."

"So be it."

He stepped into the kitchen to find her pulling a steaming pan out of the oven. As usual, handling it by the shadow meant there was no danger of burning herself, though she did toss a trivet onto the table before putting the pan down. Inside was something that defied classification for Alan. There was definitely a pastry element, so he was inclined to call it a pie, but it was quite thin and had both fruit and cheese.

"What's this?" he said.

"A fig-cheese tart." She produced a fancy pizza cutter of some kind with a scalloped edge on it and cut the tart into six pieces. "Eat. The crust is homemade, but I don't think I'm up to the task of making my own cheese yet." She crossed her arms. "Because *someone* doesn't have a big enough fridge."

"You could always try the same stunt the Shades in the sandwich shop did," Alan said, plating a piece of the tart. "Just create more shadowy room."

"Don't think I haven't tried. It would solve a *lot* of problems. We could just hide in there and not be spied on. But it takes more strength and know-how than I have to pull that particular trick off."

Alan took a bite of the tart. It was a bit fancier and more complex than he typically went for, but as far as her experiments went, it was not *so* bizarre he couldn't stomach it. "Not bad," he said. "Tell me, Blot. These breakfasts. Are you doing this for you or are you doing this for me? Because, like carrying me to bed, it's appreciated but not necessary."

She shrugged. "It's a hobby, and you're the one that has to eat. If you don't want it, I can try feeding it to Chu-chu, but you know how he is with things that aren't carrion in some way, shape, or form."

He chewed his meal and tried to grapple with his thoughts. "I feel like... I just want to make sure you're getting as much out of this as you're giving. Like you said. This is still *my* world. All things being equal, things aren't even remotely equal. The least I can do is make sure I'm not taking advantage of you."

"It's fine." Blot narrowed her eyes. "Maybe. We'll talk about it later. Right now the important thing is we never came to a conclusion last night, so we need to start working on it again."

She reached up and tapped the laptop on the counter to wake up the screen. "So far, nothing in the news to suggest anything has happened. No Shades attacking Dawn. No Dawn attacking Shades. Mostly people are still talking about the crab festival riot. Oh, look. There's that 'drone footage' we sold Cox."

"Not that it's not a relief, but why do you suppose nothing has happened yet?" Alan asked.

"I don't know. Idiots either overthinking or underthinking it," Blot said. "That's the problem with masterminds and plots and schemes. Once there's enough of them going on, you start to convince yourself that everyone out there is pulling as many strings as you are, and you start outsmarting yourself. The Shades are so dedicated to manipulation they think that everyone is doing it all the time. But we can't trust it to stay that way. So eat up and let's get going."

"Why do we need to get going?" Alan said. "Why can't we keep plotting here?"

"Because I finished the Kona blend and we need more."

"I thought we agreed one bag per week."

"Yeah, well, that's before I dragged you to bed and you woke up worried you weren't treating me right."

"... Fair."

The unusually calm morning managed to last until Alan stepped off the elevator in the parking deck.

"Fontaine."

Alan jumped and turned. The elderly leader of the local chapter of the Dawn was standing beneath the same light he'd picked before to spook Alan.

"You could just *call* me," Alan said.

"I prefer to do my business face to face. Particularly when there's cargo meant to change hands. And I've been watching the news. I imagine that trouble in Baltimore was you?"

"It was," Alan said.

"How much did you get?" he asked.

"Are we doing this now? I would have expected some place more secure, or at least more *official*."

"We don't have that sort of time. Were you able to get our equipment or not?"

"We were able to get most of it."

"I need specifics."

"All told, we're missing two books, maybe a dozen daggers, and two Shards of Shadow."

"You weren't able to get the shards?" he rumbled.

"It's a long story. Let's just say the Shades don't have them either."

He leaned on his walking stick and looked Alan in the eye.

"What are you doing?" Alan asked.

"Trying to decide if you're double-crossing me."

"What, you think I stole the shards?" Alan said.

"Yeah, planning to and succeeding to are two different things," Blot said.

"Where are the goods?" the old man said.

"In my apartment."

"Let's take a look," he said, stepping into the elevator.

"Since when is *he* invited?" Blot said.

Alan glanced at Blot with a meaningful look.

"Oh... you're thinking the protection ward can tell us if he means *us* any harm. I see. Loath as I am to trust anything the Glints put their hands on, it's served us well so far. Fine. But if he tries anything, I'm going to put a hole in his gut. Fair's fair."

Alan pressed the button, and the group rode back up to his floor. They trudged up the hallway. When they reached the door, Alan unlocked it, then stepped aside. "Do the honors," he said.

"Why? Afraid of booby traps?" the old man said.

"Humor me," Alan said.

The old man turned the knob and stepped inside, something he shouldn't have been able to do if he had violent intentions for Alan or Blot. So far so good. Alan stepped in after him and opened his bedroom closet, which was filled with several hundred pounds of recovered gear. More had been stuffed under the bed, under the couch, and in canvas sacks under the coffee table. The old man stiffly crouched and rummaged through it, eventually picking up a rather more ornate version of one of their pendants. It turned lazily on its chain.

"Either you got rid of your tagalong or you've figured out how to hide it," he said.

"That's none of your concern," Alan said.

"Mmm... Beg to differ. But I've got *bigger* concerns right now, so I'll let it slide. More importantly, you for sure don't have any of the shards stashed away. I don't care what sort of hiding you're doing, you wouldn't be able to keep me from tracking those things down. So you're at least not trying to keep them from me. It seems, impossibly, I may be able to trust you after all."

"There's more," Alan said. "I have some information for you."

"This is enough. I don't want to owe you any more than I do," the old man said, pulling out his phone.

In what was almost certainly a calculated demonstration of the additional trust Alan had earned, the man started tapping at his phone's screen without any precautions against being spied on. Blot, naturally, took full advantage of this lapse in security.

"Six-eight-six-three," she said, barking out his security code.

"Listen," Alan said. "It's important."

"He's texting someone named Grant. And he's clearly using some sort of coded language. Doesn't *quite* trust us yet," Blot said.

"They have Brink," Alan said.

The old man stopped what he was doing, then locked his phone and slipped it into his pocket. The moment his hand was free, Blot slipped her shadowy hand in after it and vanished the phone.

"They have *Brink?* I *hope* you mean his *corpse*."

"Brink is alive. He's been taken as the host for a Shade named Dun."

The mysterious Dawn member folded both hands over the end of his walking stick and thumped it against the ground. "They have Brink. Brink is alive and they have him. Horrifying. And such a profound disappointment. Brink was one of our best. Best training. Best dedication. Or so I thought. The man should have taken his life. I never would have imagined he'd allow himself to live with a Shade. It explains the leaks. We'll be able to tighten ourselves up better now. Change codes. Change procedures. Change locations."

"Keep him talking, I'm almost done," Blot said.

"We need to do something about it," Alan said.

"You don't need to do anything. This is Dawn business. You will not interfere. If you to try to do something now, if you get between us and our goal, we can't guarantee your safety."

"You'd violate the truce?" Alan said.

"You step out on a battlefield, you're the one who violated the truce."

"Hah! I've got it," Blot said, planting the phone back in his pocket. "They've been discussing how and when they'll be doing the redistribution of the gear if we got it back since the moment they asked for our help. I have all of the times and dates, and what I'm pretty sure is a coded location."

"Keep your head down," the old man said.

The box beside Alan's door buzzed.

"And that'll be some of my boys to tote this all back home."

"Are you sure you'll be able to keep it safe?" Alan said.

"Like I said, we know the nature of the leak, we'll be able to stop the bleeding. And even *with* Brink, I'd like to see them try and take what we have now. We're still the Dawn. The hard part isn't keeping it safe. The hard part is getting it back into the hands of who needs it, and that is for us to handle, not for you to so much as think about."

He marched to the door, Alan in tow.

"I hope your 'friend' appreciates the value of this truce," the old man continued. "If you two don't do something to endanger it, that thing might be the last Shade standing in this world when our work is done."

"Asserting your plan to kill the rest of my kind isn't going to make me like you any more," Blot rumbled as an unheard jab. "Let's just hurry up and get all that Shade-killing hardware out of my home."

Jessie was slightly unnerved by how easily she'd gotten permission to access Todd in prison. Particularly since she'd had to arrange for it to happen when she was intended to be off-duty, and thus had to trade shifts in order to claim she was on official police business. She offered up a rather flimsy excuse—that she thought he might have been involved with the same "gang" that was responsible for the ATM money laundering scheme. Again, *technically* true, but the number of times she'd had to qualify her truth with technicalities was beginning to curdle her soul a bit. She was going to have to walk the straight and narrow just a bit straighter and a bit narrower for a *long time* to equal out the wiggle room she'd been giving her morals lately. She didn't even allow herself to think the phrase "The ends justify the means," because that was precisely the sort of reasoning one uses to permit the most detestable of injustices.

She sat in the interview room, which still had telltale signs of recent repair after the disaster in the prison that Jessie hadn't learned the truth about until after the fact. A prison riot that was chiefly comprised of supernaturally symbiotic duos suddenly discovering they were now permanently stuck with one another tended to do a number on a prison. She would have loved to be a fly on the wall when the repair crew was working up the list of repairs, as there was a very visible bit of patchwork done to the cinder block wall that resembled a three-fingered slash of claws. Somewhere a contractor's to-do list had something like "fix the spot where Wolverine slashed the wall?" jotted down on it.

She didn't have to wait in the interview room for long. Two guards brought in Todd and threw him down into the chair. His twisted shadow, Rive, glared back at Jessie, then at Frightful on her shoulder. Frightful's shadowy form became more tense, more threatening in its posture. Her extreme distaste for non-Blot Shades was nothing if not consistent.

"Hey! Policewoman!" he said. "Didn't expect to see you here."

The words wafted across the metal folding table between them and struck her nose with a chemical sting.

"Is this man drunk?" she asked.

"Heh. No, not me," Todd said, not even attempting to hide the falseness of his claim.

"If he's getting booze in here, we haven't found his supplier," said one of the guards. "No full bottles, no empty bottles. I think this guy just drank so much over his life that it'll take fifteen years for him to dry out."

"You better hope so," Todd said. "You don't want to know me when I haven't had a drink. No fun at all."

"You want us on hand?" the first guard asked.

"Stay close, but I think I'll be able to get some freer answers out of him if we're alone," Jessie said.

"Sure thing," said the guards.

They each marched out the door. Jessie sighed.

"This all really ought to be more difficult, especially after the incident," she muttered.

"The incident. You mean the one when you cut the balls off all these Shades in here?" Todd said. "You don't know the half of what's wrong in this place."

"Shut it," said Rive. "Or no bottle tonight. You're going through them almost more quickly than I can replace them as it is."

"You call that a threat?" Todd said. "You're the one who'll have to deal with a sober me."

Rive ignored him. "How in the darkness did you find a way to tame a rikt?" he said.

"I'll ask the questions," said Jessie.

"Don't bother. You think you'll be cunning. You humans have no idea the cunning the Shades have. You thought what that *blasted* Alan Fontaine and Brink did was enough to neutralize what we'd started here? You may have left some of our soldiers weak and found a way to keep them attached to their hosts, but we know how to make lowly and worthless Shades pull their weight. Nothing you did here changed anything."

"When you told me to shut it, I thought that meant you *didn't* want the cops to know what's going on in here," Todd said.

"Oh, I want her to know. I want her to know that they had no real victory. Scattered through this prison are Shades who continue to serve our cause. Every piece of knowledge, every update, passes through this place. I know things you couldn't imagine. Things about your own world you won't learn for months. Things you won't learn until it is *far too late*. We are—"

"Enough," Jessie said. "I'm not here to give you a chance to practice your monologues. This is a questioning, and I mean to have the answers *I* am after. You claim to know things before anyone else. I assume that means you know about Baltimore."

"The traitorous Blot will pay for helping her host rob us..." he said.

"So you must know that it won't be long before the Dawn are rearmed and ready to defend themselves."

Todd laughed hoarsely.

"Something funny, sir?" Jessie said.

"Nah. Nah. I'm not saying anything. I still want the bottle tonight."

"This setback will be corrected," Rive said. "Again. It is no victory at all."

"Do you think so?" Jessie said. "As I understand it, the Dawn are spread all around the country, probably all around the world. And no leak lasts forever. Eventually those weapons will be back in their hands and you'll be back on the defensive."

"The problem is well in hand," Rive said.

"You think you can break back into the Dawn strongholds?" Jessie said. "If they have their gear back, then the keepers of that gear are the best-armed people in the world to do battle against you and yours. I find it very difficult to believe even *you* are cocky enough to risk directly assaulting a Dawn stronghold *now*. You should have struck while they were disarmed."

Todd released a hacking laugh again. "You ask me, they sapped all the fun out of it by not *having* to assault the stronghold. It's been too long since I had a decent tussle. They don't even want me in on this one."

"We know you were setting a trap. That the Dawn wasn't *nearly* as disarmed as they behaved," Rive said. "You would have loved it if we'd made our move. Thrown ourselves at a stronghold we believed to be all but harmless only to be skewered by the Dawn. But we are too wise. Too well informed. We have Brink to tell us where the strength lies. And one does not strike where someone has had time to put down roots."

"I really think it is best if you help us put an end to this fighting. We can find a way to bring peace. If a general truce is called, no one else has to die."

"Policewoman?" Todd interrupted. "I know your heart's in the right place, but his ain't. I don't know where it is, but it sure ain't in the right place. So you're really wasting your time, and to tell you the truth, I kind of get a kick out of all the talking shadows back in the cellblock. Loads of good gossip. So I'll go ahead and tell you you're wasting your breath. Nice bird shadow, though. Ain't seen too many of them around. These fellas don't seem to like 'em, and they don't seem to like these fellas."

"The fool, at least, speaks the truth. Go. Relish what time you have left. You are an enemy of the Shades now. And that comes with consequences," Rive said.

"Fine. I'll be on my way, then. But just know that you and the other Shades aren't above the law anymore. Keep your noses clean or you'll see my meaner side."

She stood and tapped the door. The guards came and collected Todd, who laughed with his boozy breath and chatted up the guards about what was on the menu that night.

"I think maybe being in a place where he's surrounded by a bunch of other Shades who are subservient to him has made him a little slack, Frightful. Because that was a bit more information than I think he meant to share."

The schedule for Alan's part-time job as a forensic photographer on call for the police department had become something of a calculus equation. For a while it was one day on, two days on call, two days off. Then it was alternate days on call, in the station once a week. Now it was one half-day per week at the station, then "call and see." Supposedly the mad scramble to do something about the ATM thefts had been draining the department's budget, and thus nonessential employees were on a sort of pseudo-furlough. All Alan knew was he'd gotten a call asking him to come do shots of an armed robbery and he'd ended up spending the next two hours in the station when he really would have preferred to be asleep. Now Alan was back home, waiting for a call from Jessie after she'd dealt with her own volatile schedule for the day. The ringing cell phone jostled him out of a half doze.

"Jessie? You okay?" he said, wiping some undignified drool from his mouth and hoping the slurring of near-sleep wasn't so obvious.

"I'm fine," Jessie said. "I haven't even taken my jacket off. So... got any cool jewelry?"

He tried to puzzle out the meaning of the question, but his mental faculties hadn't quite finished booting back up. He felt something thump into his pocket, conjured up by Blot. When he slipped his hand inside to check on it, he found the Dawn pendant there. It was quite warm. He was being watched.

"Nothing cool, I'm afraid. Maybe you'd like to talk to Blot about that thing?" he said. Until he was feeling up to being sneaky, he'd settle for being vague.

"If you don't mind," she said.

Alan held out the phone. Blot grabbed it by the shadow and pulled it into silhouette.

"You're sure your ring isn't hot?" Blot said quietly.

Alan shut his eyes and focused.

"It's only warmed up once, and it was right when I left your and Alan's apartment after he gave it to me," Jessie asked.

"Did you get that?" Blot asked.

Alan nodded, still more unsettled by the nature of his and Blot's union continuing to reveal nuances. Even though the sound of the cell phone was entirely inaudible to his *ears*, Alan could just barely hear what Jessie was saying, as though the sound was somehow traveling to him through the link that joined them.

"Let's make this quick," Alan said.

"I hear you loud and clear," Jessie said. "Now where are we?"

"The Dawn has their gear, and good riddance. The awful old man in charge showed that he's actually starting to trust us, which meant I was able to steal a peek at his phone. They don't trust us enough to speak in plain English, but there were some times and some destinations. I don't know where they took the stuff, but I think I know where they're going to take it and what times of day they consider safe to travel," Blot said. "It was like a bus schedule. They must be working around the availability of their better drivers or something."

"Times of day?" Jessie said. "Not dates and times, just times?"

"The time was pretty easy to figure out in their code because it was numbers. But there weren't any *other* numbers, so no date I could spot. So either they're moving it in a couple hours, or that same time tomorrow, or the next day. The old man also made it clear he doesn't want us involved, and if we do get involved, he won't shed a tear if we get caught in the crossfire," Blot added. "He's probably been itching for a chance to kill me and call it an accident since we escaped from him the first time."

The Shade subconsciously rubbed her gut. "I hate that guy..." she fumed. "Did you get anything?"

"Todd's handler was all bluster, but he let an awful lot slip," Jessie said. "First, I think either the Dawn is lying to you or Brink is lying to the Shades, because the Shades pretty clearly think there was still plenty of weaponry in place. A far cry from the claims of being nearly toothless that you seemed to indicate the Dawn were making."

"I don't get the feeling the old man was lying. He's not half as good at lying as he thinks he is, and that seemed pretty honest. He came off as desperate. The man's not a good enough actor to trick me like that," Blot said.

"I can't say there was any indication that the Shade shifter was trying to deceive me either. Especially because he thought *we* were trying to deceive the *Shades* about it."

"So that leaves Brink," Blot said.

"If he was lying to the Shades about how heavily armed the Dawn soldiers were, it *would* explain why they hadn't committed more effort to a real, final attack yet," Blot said.

"And he wasn't there to stop us at the sandwich shop, even though we *know* he was nearby," Alan said.

"Let me do the talking," Blot said. "We don't want them wondering why they're only getting half a conversation. But back to it. It bugs me that Brink seems like he might have a grip on this situation. Don't get me wrong, I'm not rooting for the other Shades right now. But if he's out there manipulating them, that's really disappointing. And keeping them from attacking his brethren in the Dawn by claiming they're still a legitimate threat is pretty brilliant, but it would mean he's able to lie to someone who can see his very dreams. I might be underestimating the Dawn training."

"And there's more," Jessie said. "They seemed confident they'd have the stuff you recovered back soon. And equally confident that they weren't going to 'fall into the trap' of attacking a Dawn stronghold to get it."

"Maybe they thought they were going to be getting it from my house," Alan said.

"No way," Blot said. "If they thought the apartment was a target, they would have hit us a long time ago. The Glint magic probably kept them away. It would have been more likely they would have gone for your parents, but then, the Glints have the enchantment up on their place too. I *really* don't like how much we've come to depend upon those wards. ...

But there's no way the Dawn *didn't* send it to a stronghold when they got it from us, and there's no way they won't be taking it directly *to* a stronghold whenever they decide to leave. So what exactly do the Shades think they're going to do?"

"I'm not sure," Jessie said. "They said... something about not attacking the enemy where they've put down roots, or something like that."

"Again, sounds like flowery language for a stronghold. A place they've been able to stick around long enough to be hard to move. Doesn't really teach us anything."

"Maybe," Jessie said. "But maybe there's something else to it. If we know they wouldn't hit a stronghold, what else could that mean?"

"There's no other place that's likely to have all that stuff together in one place," Blot said. "And Dun's crew wouldn't think they'd be getting it back in a hurry if they weren't planning on getting it back all at once, because if they could just hit a bunch of strongholds, they would have done it already."

"They're going to hit it in-transit," Alan said.

"Wait... wait, wait, wait..." Blot said. "Of course they are. It's so obvious. From what I saw, even through all the codes, it was pretty clear they were in a hurry to get the gear back to where it came from. So they're clearly going to move it as soon as possible. But there was only *one* set of travel instructions, coded or not. So they aren't breaking up the shipment and sending them off to all the various cells of the Dawn individually. At least, not as a part of that chain of messages. How could they? They don't have the men and women to spare to be making little deliveries all over the place from here. But they also knew they had a leak, so they knew they couldn't risk keeping it in the usual spots. So they were going to have to distribute it from somewhere else. Somewhere new. Which means they're going to have to move things, all at once, to that new place. They're going to hit them on the road..."

"My gosh," Jessie said.

"It's actually really good tactics," Blot said. "A car or truck or something, moving at high speed, is vulnerable to a well-trained Shade. I'm sure the Dawn will take steps to protect it, but no amount of protection is going to make a vehicle *as* secure as a building. Plus, a big car wreck is the kind of thing that people would accept as a standard, everyday thing. They wouldn't have to worry too much about hiding it. Just slash some tires, cause a wreck, and harvest the wreck. The Dawn'll probably have some of their burliest protectors on hand, but there's only so much you can do to protect a moving vehicle, and only so much you can do to protect yourself *in* a moving vehicle. Crash the vehicle, and the Dawn loses the goods and some of their best fighters."

"But it's obvious, isn't it?" Alan said. "Surely the Dawn are expecting it. Surely they have a plan."

"Sure they do. They must," Jessie said. "And now that they know Brink is compromised, and they must know what Brink *knew*, then they should be able to act in a way that won't be predicted by him. But there's probably only so many options available to them, and if the Shades are keeping as close an eye on them as I suspect they are, then it won't really matter."

"I don't like this," Alan said.

"Neither do I. If it's the best chance the Shades will have, even if it's obvious enough for the Dawn to see it coming, unless the Dawn are able to do the shipment entirely in secret, this is shaping up to be a bloody clash on a busy road. People are going to get hurt. Dawn, Shades, innocent people, everyone."

"I don't see how we can do anything about this," Blot said.

"... I think we need more advice," Alan said.

"Unless you've forgotten, Jessie is the only other person who knows anything about what's going on. There's no one left to get advice from. Unless you want us to go find Gladys, and the Dusk already said don't come knocking."

"No. Think about it," Alan said. "What we're looking for here is a stalemate. We want things to end roughly how they started. That's what the Glints are always after. If there's anyone who might know how to turn this into a complete wash for all involved, it's them."

"You want to ask them for help..." Blot rumbled.

"It can't hurt."

"It could most certainly hurt," Blot snapped. "But I guess it could hurt less than the consequences... Can we at least not do it here? I'm sick of them intruding on my safe spaces."

"Yeah. I think that's reasonable. Jessie, what are your plans?"

"Unless you two come up with a plan with a place in it for me, not terribly much."

"Have you changed your mind about getting the Shards of Shadow back from the Glints?" Blot asked.

"I'm not robbing a supernatural being. I'm already not entirely comfortable with the number of secret societies that are operating in this city. I'm certainly not interested in breaking laws on their behalf. But there *is* something that's been bothering me."

"What?"

"I've been thinking about the money laundering building. It's still locked down, still under investigation. But there was a whole section of the building that they'd taken *great* trouble to not just block off but attempt to completely conceal. There's still no evidence that there was anything in the locked-up stairwell. Heaps of damning evidence out in the open, but a locked-off area with nothing incriminating. It doesn't make sense. I feel like there must be something there. If there wasn't this Dawn business to deal with, I almost think it would be worth finagling the two of you into the crime scene. Make up some excuse to get the top forensic photographer in there. Because I really think Blot's expertise is called for."

"We're stretched pretty thin at the moment," Alan said.

"Granted. And by the time you aren't, I've got to imagine it'll be a cold enough investigation that getting you inside in an official capacity would be difficult."

"I could get us in in an unofficial capacity just fine," Blot said.

"No unauthorized access to crime scenes," Jessie said. "You could taint things. This is a police matter. Keep me posted. While you're doing what you have to do, I'm going to have to get back inside."

"And we'll have to head out and get the attention of the people we've been trying to avoid for this entire phone call," Blot said, shaking her head. "I am beginning to think being a servant of multiple masters is more trouble than it's worth."

CHAPTER 10

Alan and Blot were back in his car. They'd agreed, particularly in light of their recent dealings with the Glints, that it would be wise to put some distance between them while asking for advice. The only way they knew to achieve that was to seek such help while in a moving vehicle. So Alan had taken a ride around town and, when he was comfortable he was on a stretch of road where his "using the phone while driving" rule could once again be bent, he reached into his pocket and wrapped his hand around the Dawn pendant that Blot had applied an additional enchantment to. It was just a bit warmer than his pocket should have made it. They were being watched.

"It's time," Alan said.

"Let me see if I can ease the stealth enchantment. That ought to make it obvious."

Alan couldn't quite tell what Blot's motions translated to, but after a moment, she eased a hand out of the shadows, popped the glove compartment open, and produced a slip of paper to stow inside.

"Now," she said.

Alan cleared his throat. "Angel, if you have a minute I'd like a word with—"

The phone rang, interrupting him.

"—you," he muttered.

Blot took the phone and put it on speaker.

"Alan! Dina and Gabriel tell me you did a wonderful job at the sandwich shop," they said.

"Yeah, I'll bet they did," Blot grumbled.

"Listen, I need your help," said Alan.

"I am not typically one who offers help when it is requested. I'm more of an observer, you see."

"You're an observer who wants to maintain *balance*, right?" Alan said.

"That is our goal... as humans," Angel said, as if there was some maximum amount of time they would allow to pass without asserting their humanity.

"Then listen up. The Shades and the Dawn are probably about to slaughter each other."

"Either in a few hours or the next day at that time. Maybe the day after that," Blot said.

"Soon," Alan summarized. "And that would put the gear *right* back into the Shade's hands."

"That *does* appear to be the most likely outcome presently," Angel said.

"That doesn't strike me as a terribly balanced outcome."

"It is our determination that the attack will take the lives of quite a few of the Shades and hosts along with the Dawn. And according to Dina and Gabriel, external factors are in place that will tilt the scales to offset any disproportionate Shade gains."

"What? How? What sort of offset?" Alan said.

"That isn't for you to know. It, evidently, isn't for *me* to know, either. They have been away since shortly after your successful mission."

"There must be something we can do to have a balanced scale *without* wholesale slaughter."

"Quite possibly. There are a number of outcomes that we would consider to be equally appropriate, and several may have been achievable without any guaranteed bloodshed. But those would have required significant interference, and we've already asked so much of you. We do like to keep our touch light."

"Yeah, they really have some light fingers," Blot said.

"What's the plan?"

"I shall tell you, but only because it is superfluous and largely irrelevant at this point. A potential stalemate could have been achieved by accelerating the delivery of the equipment through your own means, and delivering a warning to both the Dawn regarding the precise timing of a prospective attack, and to the Shades regarding the danger of launching such an attack."

"That sounds like a workable plan. Let's do it," Alan said.

"Unnecessary and irrelevant, as I've said."

"Considering me and Blot would be the ones putting our necks on the line, I think that's up to us to decide, isn't it?"

"For the superfluous part, but not the irrelevant one. Because, you see, you're too late."

"Too late?!" Alan said, looking at Blot.

"No, no. Even if they were making the move today, the time was *hours* from now."

"Blot says she saw the earliest planned departure time as a couple hours in the future," Alan said.

"Had it not occurred to her that when planning a rendezvous for any reason, it is the *arrival* time that must be shared, not the departure time?"

"I... You..." Blot slapped her head. "Stupid, stupid, stupid." Her shadowy hands rose up to fiddle with the phone, brought up a maps app, and punched in a destination.

"Can you see the destination Blot just punched in?"

"Heavens, no. But were I to speculate, it would be a warehouse in Pittsburgh."

"That's a five-hour drive, at least," Alan said. "When's the arrival time supposed to be?"

"Five thirty p.m.," Blot said.

Alan checked the clock. It was ten minutes to two. The Dawn had more than an hour head start. He leaned on the accelerator and eyed the on-ramp to the highway.

"Alan, I request that you refrain from risking yourself in this way. You are a useful fellow, and I would prefer you remain a viable agent when needed."

"Your concern is touching, but I have lives to save," Alan said.

"Very well, I can't stop you over the phone. But I hope you realize I'll have to keep an eye on you even more closely until you are out of danger, if only to know that you are not going to cause us problems."

"I'll try to live with the guilt," Alan said.

Blot hung up the phone, then subtly pulled the phone into the darkness. A less subtle click of the glove compartment fetched the paper enchantment so that she could reassert their stealth. "I'm going to let Jessie know," Blot said.

Alan nodded. He wasn't thrilled about giving her something new to worry about, but it was better she knew.

Jessie stepped under the police caution tape and clicked on her flashlight. Because the building was part of her regular beat anyway, and she'd been a part of the bust, it hadn't been *too* difficult to arrange permission to have an additional look around the former site of the money laundering ring.

The evidence had all been collected. Considering how much of that evidence consisted of stray twenty-dollar bills, the scouring of the building was *particularly* thorough. Thus, she didn't anticipate finding anything natural lurking about in the locked stairwell. If there was anything to find, it would be found in shadow or via her rikt's instincts.

"I don't know how well you understand me, Frightful, but if you're getting any notions, don't keep them a secret."

In the darkness, with her flashlight as the only decent light source, the rikt wasn't terribly visible to her. She couldn't feel the thing curled in her shadow, and she *could* feel its phantom talons dug into her arm, so she knew it was on her shoulder. But that meant she'd have to shine the flashlight on herself and look behind her to look the beast in the eye. Better to listen and feel, while keeping her eyes trained on the ground for clues.

She walked the full stairwell from bottom to top, but nothing jumped out at her—literally or figuratively—during the trip. Again, because the investigation had been so thorough, she pulled a printout of the police report from her pocket, hoping to spot inconsistencies. There was nothing apparent. But on the walk back down from the top floor, she felt Frightful growing progressively more restless. By the time she reached the lower level, where she'd originally discovered the blocked stairwell, Frightful was starting to inch forward, fighting the edge of the flashlight's beam to reach... something.

Jessie crouched and tugged at the utility panel. When it swung open, she found the inside just as unremarkable as it was before. But Frightful was *very* interested. Jessie fished a handkerchief out of her pocket and draped it over the front of the flashlight to dim its beam. Frightful quickly took advantage in a way that, in retrospect, Jessie should have predicted. She felt the talons ease their grip on her shoulder and there was a brief flitting black form across the dimmed beam that vanished from her view the moment the last talon had tugged away.

"No, no, no. Frightful, come back. Come. Come Frightful," she said urgently.

This, of all places, was *not* the sort of place she would have wanted to find herself without the ability to see Shades. As if to hammer home how vulnerable she suddenly felt, a muffled grinding sound she couldn't identify sent her hand to the grip of her gun, as though somehow she'd be able to protect herself if a supernatural entity had chosen this moment to strike.

The grinding continued, then the tingle of talons returned to her shoulder.

"Oh, thank goodness," she said, reaching up to try to offer a scratch to Frightful. "Don't scare me like that, sweetie."

The rikt, for the moment, forwent the scratches to instead focus intently on the seemingly unremarkable utility cabinet. Slowly, an inky figure started to ease out from a previously unseen gap between the floor and the wall. Jessie scrambled backward, debating pulling the hanky from the flashlight to force whatever it was back. She thought better of it. She wouldn't learn anything if she didn't stand her ground and see what she was dealing with. And Frightful was uncharacteristically calm. Considering how surly she acted around Shades besides Blot, if she wasn't posturing, this wasn't a Shade that should concern her.

The figure was quite large and lanky, a Shade that offered only the briefest glance in Jessie's direction, choosing instead to focus on Frightful. At first, Jessie thought it didn't have any limbs, but it turned out the Shade had simply folded its arms in front of its body. The reason it had done so became clear the moment it chose to unfold them again.

A second figure popped up out of the darkness like a beach ball that had been forced below the surface. It was... a child. He couldn't be older than six. He had Asian features and looked quite dirty and quite frightened. He squinted at the light, first frightened, then relieved.

"Are you a police?" said the little boy.

"Yes. Do you need help?" she said, crouching down.

"Where are we?" he said.

It was painfully clear that the little boy was at the very brink of tears. That he was holding it together was almost more heartbreaking to Jessie than his weeping would have been, because it meant this boy was no stranger to holding back tears.

"You're at the corner of Park and Oxford."

"Where?" he said, no hint of understanding.

"Philadelphia," she said.

"Where?" he repeated.

"Pennsylvania."

The boy lowered his eyes to address the Shade. "Did we go far?" he said.

"We went far," said the Shade in a feminine voice.

The voice was more distant and labored than when Blot spoke. This Shade was either weak or injured.

"Where are you from?" Jessie asked the Shade directly.

The Shade eyed her uncertainly, then glanced at her feet, as if to interrogate her shadow.

Jessie tipped her head toward the rikt. "Frightful here lets me see what's going on."

"You've tamed a rikt?" the Shade said. "I've never seen one here. Only back home. They say they show up when someone is nearly... When someone..." The Shade glanced at the boy, seemingly choosing her words with care for the sake of the child. "When one is nearly ready to move on," the Shade said. "And you've *tamed* it?"

"Not tamed. Just... we've come to an agreement. Please, where did you come from?" Jessie said.

"Buffalo," the Shade said.

"Buffalo, New York?" she said.

The little boy nodded.

"How long ago?"

"A few minutes," the Shade said.

"That's hundreds of miles away."

"It's... we..." the Shade stuttered.

"Listen. I'm not here to hurt anyone. And clearly the boy needs help. If you come clean with me, I'll do what I can to make sure you are taken care of."

Jessie briefly considered assuring them she had a Shade as a friend, but she wasn't sure Blot would strictly agree with that assessment. And more to the point, she wasn't sure having Blot as a friend would be of any use in convincing a Shade to trust her if the others had been pushing a reputation of infamy. As it so happened, the boy made the Shade's decision for her.

"It's a fast way. A tunnel," the boy said.

"A tunnel," Jessie said, uncertain. "Honey, a tunnel wouldn't make a three-hundred-mile trip fast enough to cover in a few minutes. Unless..." She glanced at the Shade. "This is some sort of Shade shortcut, isn't it?" she said. "It would explain why this area was blocked off. They didn't want anyone to discover their little highway."

"I should deny it, but what's the point anymore? They have the light. The Burning Light," the Shade said fearfully. "The end is near. The rikt was right to come."

"The end of what?" the little boy said.

"What is the Burning Light? And who has it?" Jessie asked.

"It's bright!" the boy said. "And it hurt Murk bad."

"You would be Murk?" Jessie said to the Shade.

The Shade nodded.

"So the Burning Light is a weapon," Jessie said.

"A terrible one. I barely made it out alive. It killed so many of us. If you can protect us, then I accept any terms," Murk said.

"Killed Shades? When?" Jessie said.

181

"It's what sent us south through the tunnel. I... I think we're the only ones that made it through before the other opening was burned away. If it wasn't for the presence of the rikt to head toward, I don't think we would have found our way out. It wasn't ready to be used yet. There was no guidance to traverse it."

"How many were killed?" Jessie said, now fully in "Officer Hearst" mode.

"There were thirty-five of us. At least half must be dead, if not more."

"You're telling me over a dozen Shades, and presumably their hosts, were killed in the Buffalo area just a few minutes ago?" Jessie said.

"Yes," Murk confirmed.

Jessie pinned the dimmed flashlight under her arm and fetched her phone. To her horror, social media was just starting to light up with reports, and the very earliest of speculative bits of coverage were starting to flow in the local news. "Ten bodies were discovered, all recently deceased with no signs of violence or foul play. Police have evacuated the area, concerned about a possible gas leak or other unidentified toxin."

She looked up from the phone and pocketed it. Once she'd returned the flashlight to one hand, she hefted the boy from the ground.

"Come on. Let's get you to the squad car. Do you know where your parents are?"

"They were... they were with the others," the little boy said.

"You took a whole family?" Jessie said coldly, glaring at the Shade being cast from the boy.

"We did what we were ordered to. We obey Stigma," Murk said.

"Stigma. I've heard that name before." She started to climb the stairs. "Tell me about the Burning Light."

"It shouldn't work here. It would take too much strength to bring it about. And it only hurts Shades. We wouldn't want to summon it even if we could."

"It's Shade magic?"

"Yes."

"Could someone else cast Shade magic?"

"Only if they had a source of our power."

"Like a Shard of Shadow?" Jessie said.

"You know a great deal about our kind," Murk said.

"Apparently not enough to make a proper decision," she said.

Jessie's mind sizzled with the realization that it was very possible this was the work of the Glints, and quite possibly by using one of the items she'd been tasked with reclaiming from them. If that was so... a dozen or more lives were lost because she'd failed to do so.

She had to call the others, to find out more. But something told her this was going to change things.

This was going to change everything.

Over the last few hours, Alan had racked up more time driving over the speed limit than the rest of his life combined. Blot had been doing her level best to stretch her slowly developing mystic senses to detect the contents of the van. The Dawn weapons weren't terribly substantial in their enchantment, but there were a *lot* of them, and Blot was quite familiar with them after having shared an apartment with them for a day. They were getting close, close enough that Alan had begun eying every potential truck or van as a possible Dawn vehicle. But even without Blot's magic, Alan knew he was close, because of the sky.

"Look at those clouds..." he murmured.

There was a storm brewing. Already the rain was falling in sheets. But this was no natural storm. He'd never seen clouds so dark, or ones that had formed with such a sharp, defined edge.

"This is Shade magic, isn't it."

"I didn't know we could do that, but there's no doubt in my mind. The power someone is pumping into those clouds... there must be twenty high-skill Shades focusing all their strength to fuel that storm. And they must be *very* close. But I still can't see any, can you?"

"No. But I—" Alan began.

His phone rang. Blot fetched it.

"It's Jessie," Blot said.

"Answer it. It could be important," Alan said.

Blot subtly pulled the phone into the shadows with her. "What is it?" she said. "Alan's driving."

"Blot. Just the person I needed to talk to," Jessie said. "What do you know about the Burning Light?"

"What do *you* know about the Burning Light?" Blot said suspiciously.

"I've encountered a Shade named Murk who claims to have barely survived being exposed to Burning Light."

"Murk?" Blot said. "You've encountered Murk."

"Yes. She's right here in the squad car with me. I'm heading back to the precinct with her host, a little boy named Bo."

"Murk is a scribe of Stigma," Blot said. "Murk would never be anywhere Stigma *isn't*. And would tear you to pieces if you got anywhere close to him."

"She is alone. And I don't think she'll be tearing anyone to pieces anytime soon. She's very weak. She looks thin, and the edge of her shadow is, I don't know, crispy for lack of a better word. She's trying to tell you something, but I can barely hear her when she speaks, so I doubt it's coming across the phone."

"What's she saying?" Blot said.

"She's... um... let's just say she's not very fond of you."

"Does *she* say it was Burning Light?"

"She does."

Alan spared a brief glance in her direction. "Anything I need to know? I can't quite hear her right now."

"In a minute. Jessie's making some claims that are impossible. You can't *do* the Burning Light here. It's Shade magic, and there's just no way a Shade here would be able to use it safely. They'd be consumed in it just as surely as the Shades around them."

"I don't think it was the Shades who used it. It seems it was used against a large group of Shades. I doubt they would have done it to themselves. I think a Shard of Shadow was involved," Jessie said.

"I guess a Shard of Shadow *could* fuel it for a non-Shade, and it certainly wasn't the Dawn that used it. If the Dawn had access to the Burning Light, they would have been using it against us since the start. But the Glints have shards, we know that, and they've been targeting Stigma."

"My thoughts exactly," Jessie said.

Blot glanced at Alan. "So the Glints almost certainly have found a way to produce the Burning Light. And they've used it to kill how many people?"

"A dozen or more," Jessie said.

"More than a dozen dead. You getting all this, Alan?"

"I am," he said with forced steadiness.

"Jessie, you have to get the shards away from them," Blot said. "Laws or no. The Burning Light... I can't think of a human weapon that even comes close. It's like they're out there spraying acid on people."

"I only wish I'd known the stakes before, I could have tried to prevent this. But what do I do now? It isn't as though there's a front door I can just knock on."

"There *is* one. Angel's front door. It's... Blast it, we've *seen* it... They did something to push it out of our heads time and time again. I just... wait. Wait, there's the pages the Dusk gave us. What did they say? If you can't find something and you believe it was taken from you, you can prove it to yourself by looking for the gaps. Alan, help me out here. They tinkered with *your* head more directly than mine. Where's the door they're hiding? And don't say it directly if you get it, we don't want them to know we know. I'm still not entirely sure how much they can still detect from you even with the stealth enchantment in full force."

"It's... Um... I don't... Give me a minute," Alan said.

"Regardless of where it is, if it's hidden from you, surely it's hidden from *me*," Jessie said.

"Maybe so, but if you can figure out which door it is, that ring we enchanted for you *should* allow you to get in. Or at least that's what the Dusk's notes said, remember? By the void, I hope they know what they are talking about..."

"Name our neighbors," Alan said.

"Name our neighbors," Blot repeated. "There's Mrs. Levitt next door and... Jessie, Angel's door is the one directly across from us. It's labeled something other than an apartment number."

"Are you sure?" Jessie said.

"I'm sure, because I'm not sure. And something I see every day is something I should be sure of," Blot said.

"All right. I'm heading over there as soon as I get this child somewhere safe," Jessie said. "If you don't hear from me soon..."

"Listen. You don't have a Shade and you've survived the prison uprising, you've chased off a whole apartment building full of Shades. You're going to pull this off," Blot said. "Get this done. Lives hang in the balance."

"On the right, just past the guardrail," Alan said suddenly.

Blot slid up the seat and looked out the window. A Shade, presumably having pulled its host into the shadows, was being pushed along by the headlights of a car just ahead of them, swerving around pools of glare on the rain-soaked road.

"Looks like we both have a job to do. Because whatever is going to happen is going to happen *now*," Blot said.

Chapter 11

A lan pulled over to the side of the highway. It was clear they wouldn't solve this problem without leaving the vehicle, and doing that at highway speeds was unacceptable. The rain was downright apocalyptic, so much so that several other cars *without* supernatural missions to carry out were *also* pulled over.

"Are we ready?" Blot said.

"As ready as I'll ever be," Alan said.

"Not yet you're not," Blot said.

She produced a GoPro and eased herself out of the shadows to use entirely too many zip ties to affix it to the same overengineered headband as the headlamp he'd taken to wearing at times like this.

"Seriously?" Alan said.

"I've got one and so does Chu-chu. If this is going to get exciting, we're going to have *loads* of coverage for Cox. No sense leaving money on the table when we risk our lives."

Alan shook his head and wiped the water from his eyes, but, he was disappointed to discover, did not feel compelled to remove the GoPro. He huffed and puffed a few times, then held his breath. Blot waited until a car passed, then yanked him into the shadows just as the headlights of the next one were approaching. The light struck them like a firehose, forcing them forward to surf along at highway speeds without a vehicle. If it wasn't both a near-death experience *and* one that could cost the lives of countless others if they failed, Alan might have reveled in this moment. Every long car ride of his childhood, he'd burned away the boredom by staring out the window and imagining he was some sort of action hero, jumping from roof to roof on the cars around him. Now they were doing precisely that, albeit in a way he'd lacked the creativity to imagine at the time. Blot pulled and swerved, steering the pair into the wake of the headlights of whichever car was moving fastest in this veritable monsoon. Slowly they started to ease past the Shade taking a more stealthy approach along the side of the road.

Alan's lungs started to burn and urge him to take a breath. He fought them, trying to will himself into believing that he *didn't* have to breathe despite what his body told him. His body barely existed at all right now. It shouldn't be calling the shots.

They crept closer to the van they'd suspected belonged to the Dawn. It was a contractor van with what must have been every aftermarket lighting rig available bolted to the front. It was riding a little low. The gear they'd delivered wouldn't quite account for that much weight. They must have had at least four burly defenders in there as well, though from their point of view while skimming along the pavement, they couldn't be certain.

"There's another four Shades approaching from ahead," Blot said. "No... Six... *Ten?* That one riding along behind must have been there to distract them, keep their detectors pointed in its direction. We need to do this *now*. Hold on."

It was a symbolic instruction, as there wasn't a whole heck of a lot Alan could do *besides* hold on. Blot held him as firmly as she could with one hand and poked the claws of the other hand up into reality, grinding along the roadside. It started to slow them down, forcing them deeper and deeper into the powerful shine of the headlights of the driver whose lack of consideration in keeping his high beams on had provided them with their current velocity. When the pressure of the light was almost unbearable, she released her claws and they were launched forward like they'd been fired from a slingshot. They just barely reached the back door of the van. Blot cast them up along the windowless door and attempted to tease herself between the gap.

"It's no good. They must be blasting some seriously bright light inside. It's pushing me out."

Alan's mind-over-matter approach to oxygen deprivation was quickly failing, and he was clawing at the arms holding him in the darkness.

"Um... Um... Please find a way to hold on so we don't die, Alan," Blot said.

Before Alan could work out what plan could possibly have inspired that statement, she slid them onto the roof and... released him.

He emerged from the shadows on the top of the van, facing the rear, and reflexively scrambled to grab the roof rack intended to secure a ladder to the roof. The wind whistled in his ears, and his heart tried to burrow its way out of his chest to freedom, but the fear of death was a potent motivation to keep his fingers locked tight around the rack.

"No! No, no, no, no!" he raved, unable to wrestle anything more logical from his panicked brain.

He could just barely hear similarly startled shouts from inside as the Dawn realized they had an unexpected passenger.

"Release Chu-chu!" Blot said.

"I need both hands to *not die*!" Alan shouted.

"You're doing fine! Just hold on!" Blot shouted. She pulled the stone from Alan's pocket. "Chu-chu-chu!" she trilled. "It's time to protect Mommy and Daddy!"

She knocked the stone on the roof. The sprite form of the rikt peeled off and jumped to the shadow of one of the struts of the roof rack. After an adorable yawn, it noticed the swarming Shades in the distance and unfurled into her typical form before darting down the side of the van, squawking a violent challenge to the approaching foes.

"Blot, I need to get inside!" Alan barked over the whipping wind. "My hands are going numb!"

"It's too bright in there. I'd been planning on them stopping when you showed up on the roof so we could reason with them."

"You *planned this*?!"

"No time to argue! The one thing we have going for us is that the headlights mean they can't attack from ahead, and all the Shades attacking have hosts, so they're limited in what they can do without surfacing and can only stay under for so long. I need to get down there to fend them off."

Blot cast herself down the side of the van, fighting the light from the neighboring cars. A bulky, powerful Shade whisked toward the van, claws beginning to emerge. She heaved herself at it, bashing the Shade far enough away for the headlights of Mr. High Beams to shove it to the median of the highway. An almost-joyful screech from Chu-chu erupted from beneath the van, and the rikt rebounded off another Shade, knocking them away.

The drivers of the van finally got the hint that some additional precautions might be called for and switched on the massive lighting rig. The road ahead lit up like high noon, parting a swarm of Shades that were charging toward them.

"Listen! Old man! If you are in there, *the* Shades *know!* You need help and we can give it! Just, for god's sake, let me in!" Alan bellowed from the roof.

The back door of the van flew open, spilling the painfully bright light from inside onto the road behind and pushing away a pair of Shades attempting to overtake them from behind. The scattering of remaining cars on the road wisely started to give the van some space. Without nearby cars to push them forward with their headlights, the Shades that fell behind *remained* behind, unable to match the speed of the van. Coupled with the blasting light rig on the front, only the sides of the van were vulnerable.

The old man leaned out of the back of the van, holding tight to a strap and peering up at the unwanted passenger above.

"Care to explain yourself before I have my men shake you off the roof and out of my hair?"

"This van is surrounded by Shades!" Alan shouted.

"The only Shade we are detecting was well behind us."

"*I'm* here. Are you detecting one above you? They've gotten *very* good at stealth."

The van swerved and rumbled across the uneven road surface. Alan held so tight he could hear his knuckles cracking over the wind and rain. The old man, who remained unnervingly calm given the fact he was leaning out the back of a moving van, looked down and saw what were clearly multiple furrows dug into the cement in the form of three-fingered claw marks.

"What do we see up ahead?" he shouted.

"We've got a shifter on the median. It just slashed its way across the road."

"How did they find out about where we were going?" the old man demanded.

"*I'm on the roof of a van on the highway, I'm done answering questions!*" Alan raved.

"Brace yourself!" shouted the driver.

"What now?!" Alan yelped.

He turned and saw, for an instant, one of the shifters at the base of one of the high-tension transmission towers. The shadow had twisted the human into something akin to the big-eyed ogres he'd narrowly avoided clashing with in Baltimore. It was hammering at the base of the tower with the twisted remains of a section of guardrail torn from the roadside.

"Oh god no..." Alan breathed.

An apocalyptic creak of bending metal split the air, and for an instant, the stormy highway was awash in the brightest light Alan had ever seen. He heard Blot and half a dozen other Shades at various distances cry out in pain as the light hammered them to the ground. A moment later, the tower came crashing down behind them. More screeching metal prompted tires to screech as well, a second tower already teetering barely two hundred yards ahead of the van. The old man was tossed into the van by the sudden stop. Alan's grip gave out, and he slid across the roof and tumbled down the windshield. He failed to shatter it, and probably would have fractured his skull on the asphalt if a woozy Blot hadn't pulled him down into the shadows rather than letting him strike the ground. They streaked forward, riding the powerful lights until Blot was able to slow them enough to allow him to emerge on the wet street without smearing Alan to a paste.

The combined fear of being electrocuted by downed lines during a rainstorm and being torn in half by whatever Shade got to him first was a potent incentive for Alan to get his head straight. He gasped a breath and shakily held his hand down. Blot handed him a weatherproof camera out of the shadows, and he clicked the flash into the charge position. It whined like a sci-fi weapon activating. He got his bearings. Six members of the Dawn emerged from the van. Four of them were as beefy and imposing as Brink, each wielding a silver dagger in one hand and an unidentified and vaguely arcane device of some kind in the other. The things looked like crossbows. Though, rather than strings there were gleaming silver wires, and he couldn't make out any actual bolts loaded into them. The old man stood with his walking stick, radiating the fearlessness of someone who had already lived a decade longer than he'd ever intended to and saw death as an overdue appointment rather than something to concern himself with.

The erratic driving in the minutes prior had persuaded what little traffic remained on the storm-besieged road to back off or speed away already, so for the moment, the only vehicle corralled by fallen metal towers, guardrails, and tangled wires was the Dawn's van itself.

Alan raised the camera and snapped a sequence of pictures, knocking the slowly rising combat forms of the Shades back to the pavement and further documenting the chaos on the off chance he'd survive long enough to sell the higher-quality photos to Cox as well.

"This is not going according to plan, Alan," Blot said.

"Fontaine!" the old man shouted. "If you're on our side, *get* on our side. Because we're about to light this place up."

Alan snapped a few more pictures to give himself enough cover to reach the van. Heavy-duty ship lights were being thumped down, each with their own chunky batteries. One by one, they were snapped on. Blot and all the other Shades were plastered to the ground. Alan was able to get inside the ring of lights, backing against the van to let Blot cast herself against it.

"What's your play?" the old man said.

"You saw what just happened to me, do you think we're anywhere near a plan that I would have devised?" Alan said. "What's *your* plan?"

"We were supposed to be making stops along the way to our final destination, dropping parcels of weaponry to cells waiting for us, before the main redistribution is at the end of the line."

One of the Dawn pulled the trigger of his gadget. The silver wire dragged across the top of the crossbow body, and a burst of sparks flung from the tip. It may as well have been a shotgun blast, judging by the reactions of the Shades. Angry shadows barked orders to their human hosts to stay clear of the sparks. The enemies took cover, at least for now.

"We have a strike team, one of the very teams stripped of their gear by prior heists, just a few miles away."

"Call them in!" Alan said.

Another pair of shots kept the shifters and human hosts honest.

"They're unarmed! The weapons they were meant to wield are *in the van*. They'd be torn to pieces if they tried to help us without their equipment."

"Alan, duck!" Blot shouted.

He hit the ground without a moment of thought. A scattering of slung stones dented the side of the van. None of them struck Alan, but, crucially, one of them *did* strike the light stand that had been set up. While the Dawn had invested in lights that could withstand that sort of punishment, it still fell down, and in doing so, it opened a direct path of darkness. Huddled, crouching hosts sank into the shadows and streaked along this darkened avenue as one of the members of the Dawn scrambled to right the light. One of the attacking Shades slashed at him, gashing his leg and knocking him back. Another tried to drag the unsteady man into the shadows. Blot slashed at the Shade, releasing the man from its clutches. In the blink of an eye, three of the other Shades had converged upon her. She shrieked in pain and anger as they tried to tear her free from Alan. He snapped a picture, but one of the Shades managed to just barely resist the flash.

Another member of the Dawn leveled his crossbow, ready to blast the ground where he assumed the Shades must be. Alan shoved the tip of the weapon away.

"You'll hit Blot!" he shouted.

"If we don't do something, we're *all* done for," the old man shouted. "Blades out. Carve the ground!"

A horrifying shriek rang out from beneath the van, one that startled not just Alan but the members of the Dawn too. A piercing white eye amid the darkness beneath the van darted forward. The form of a monstrous avian beast was just barely discernable among the roiling, scrambling Shades. Evidently, Chu-chu wasn't fond of the idea of someone hurting Blot.

The monstrous combat form of the rikt managed to straddle the line between the shadows and the physical world. It was like a shark gliding along the surface of the ground, rippling as pure inky darkness. It tore the other Shades away from Blot, then lurched fully out of the shadows just as Blot did in *her* combat form.

It threw its beak wide and shrieked a bone-shaking challenge to the other Shades.

"What the *hell* is that thing?" the old man said.

"That's Chu-chu. He's on our side. And it's good to know all those treats haven't been going to waste."

The sight of the beast was more than enough to convince even the shifters that it was, perhaps, not wise to draw any closer.

"Any idea if Chu-chu can stay like this for long?" Alan whispered to Blot.

"A couple minutes," she said.

"Any chance you can persuade him to stay here and protect the Dawn?" Alan said.

"Sure I can. Chu-chu is whip-smart. I always said that. Also he really hates other Shades, and there's loads of them for him to 'play with,' so I think he'll want to stick around."

Alan turned to the old man. "Tell me exactly where the strike team is and give me enough gear to arm them. I'll get it to them and come back with reinforcements."

"You're asking us to trust a wild Shade creature we've never even heard of to help protect us?" the old man said.

"Do you have any better ideas?"

The two men stared each other down. Chu-chu dug his claws into the ground, prompting a hidden Shade attempting to get the drop on them to retreat, groaning in pain.

Without looking, the Dawn leader addressed one of the heavies behind him. "Give him the duffel bag."

At least eighty pounds of bagged-up gear hit Alan's chest, nearly knocking him to the ground.

"Address on the tag. Make it fast." The old man turned to the others. "We don't know how long we're going to have to hold out, so conserve bow shots. Daggers down, lights bright, eyes wide. Let that... *thing* do the fighting for now."

"Chu-chu," Blot said, "do a good job and we'll figure out how to get you a whole pig! And Alan, threaten the Dawn for me, would you. I don't want them 'accidentally' hurting Chu-chu once the Shades are beaten back."

Alan took a few deep breaths. "If Chu-chu shows any Dawn scars when we come back, I will be *very* disappointed," Alan said.

"Weak," Blot said, yanking him and the bag into the shadows to begin their slide toward the reinforcements.

Jessie reached Alan's floor and marched toward his apartment's door. One hand was nervously in her pocket, her mind focused on the silver ring on her finger. It felt heavy, unfamiliar. But it didn't feel warm. She wasn't being watched. She shouldn't have been surprised. If there was one thing Alan and Blot could do, it was make a spectacle.

She stopped at his door and turned to the one opposite it. Contrary to their claims, it didn't seem to be anything arcane or mystical. It was a utility room of some kind. But they knew this madness better than she did. She stared down the sign, as if she could will it into revealing its secrets. But

Utility it remained. She turned to Alan's door, then to the others along the hallway.

"Clever..." she said.

The numbering system didn't make sense. There was a number missing. She turned back to the door.

"The enchantment will let you through... The enchantment will let you through... Time to become either a secret hero or a public disgrace."

She took a deep breath, took a step back, and drove her heel into the deadbolt above the door. The door frame splintered. A second kick got the door to swing open, revealing the impossible.

It wasn't an apartment. It wasn't a utility room. It was some sort of library, or cathedral. Lit with warm, bright candles and awash with white marble and gold detailing.

"My god..." she murmured.

Frightful croaked uncomfortably and slipped from her shoulder. Before her influence fully left Jessie, she was able to spot the rikt coiling underneath the door to Alan's apartment.

"That's not the best sign," she muttered.

"Hey!" came a familiar shout from behind her.

She turned to find Mrs. Levitt. She looked like she was all worked up, ready to unload one of her all-too-frequent tirades, but at the sight of the open door, her eyes were narrowed and unfocused. It was the look of someone trying and failing to look into the sun. She lingered for a moment, then stepped back into her apartment, locking it behind her.

"Powerful magic," Jessie remarked.

Uncertain of just how long she'd be able to access this place without resistance, she stepped inside the "apartment."

"I swore I'd never carry Dawn weapons again, and here I am," Blot fumed, dragging Alan through the shadows as quickly as she could manage. "I can feel them knocking against me through that bag. I'm going to feel like one big bruise after this."

Getting past the Shades around the van had been easier than she'd expected. Chu-chu had seen to that. But getting past them and losing them were two very different processes. Alan's frequent trips through the shadows had been steadily building his prowess at interpreting the world in this bizarre, altered way. He could see the wisps of black that formed the pursuing Shades.

On the disturbingly short list of things that were working in their favor, the pursing Shades weren't gaining any ground. It was plain to Alan that the attackers were selected for their combat prowess, not their speed. Only one Shade seemed to be keeping pace, and Alan suspected it was the same one that had been serving as the distraction, surfing along the headlights on the highway.

But they were far from the highway now. So far, in fact, that the unnatural storm was behind them and the late afternoon sun was a constant obstacle. Blot popped Alan out of the shadows and he hit the ground at a sprint, huffing out his expended breath and sucking in a fresh one. He sprinted across the well-lit streets of a city somewhere in the seemingly endless sequence of little towns dotted across his home state that he'd never, ever heard of. The power was out, and the sun was frustratingly

THE CLASH OF SHADOWS

angled in the wrong direction to rush them toward their goal. Thus, their journey to the Dawn drop-off spot for the strike team had turned into alternating dashes by Alan across bright open spaces and blisteringly fast jaunts through shaded stretches. His phone was in his hand, the navigation app desperately trying to figure out if he was driving or walking.

"Two more miles northwest," he panted.

He made it across the street and practically dove into the shadows like they were a swimming pool. Long gone were the fears that he might be spotted doing such things. He was just going to have to depend upon the human mind's capacity to ignore what it had seen when those sightings were suitably inexplicable.

A half mile of avenue streaked by as they swam through the shadows of a line of storefronts. Then they took another sprint across the street that nearly got Alan smeared across the pavement by a delivery truck and back into the shadows.

"I really hope these Dawn guys aren't dumb enough to put up a fight, because if one more person we're trying to help takes a swing at me, I'm going to tear their shadow off as a treat for Chu-chu," Blot promised. "He *deserves* something tasty after this."

They reached the next intersection, and it became instantly clear where they were headed. In the center of large, sparsely populated parking lot, another van much like the one trapped on the highway was parked and waiting, with Dawn members just barely visible through the windshield.

Blot released Alan, and he bobbed up to start the sprint toward the members of the Dawn.

"Please don't shoot me, please don't shoot me, please don't shoot me," he huffed to himself, knowing full well that right now he was an inexplicably soaking-wet man in torn clothes running like he was being pursued by an ax-wielding maniac while no such attacker was in sight.

One of the van doors opened. Words flooded out of him with exhausted gasps taking the place of punctuation.

"I have a package from your boss!" he shouted. "He's a man in blue with silver buttons but he needs your help and I can tell you where but right now someone's probably going to try to kill all of us you've got to trust me!"

"Whoa, whoa, whoa," said one of the members of the Dawn as he got closer. "I don't know who you think you are or what you think you're doing, but you'd better—"

Alan stumbled against the car beside the van and eyed the intersection he'd come from. A thin, middle-aged man—similarly soaking wet, similarly winded, and with a haunted look that was easily explained by the twisted shadow he cast—emerged from an alley.

"My name is Alan Fontaine. I have a Shade, and *we* have a truce. Right now the old man who I think is your boss is pinned on the highway in the middle of the same collapsed section of the power grid that caused the power outage. He's besieged by Shades, one of which is attached to that man."

"Do you have a camera strapped to your head?" said a member of the Dawn, doubtful.

"Yes. But you know what else I have?" He nodded. An eighty-pound duffel slid out from the shadow of the car. "I have hardware."

"I can't believe we're taking help from a Shade," rumbled one of the other members of the Dawn, who fortunately seemed aware that Alan

Fontaine was indeed on the "don't necessarily kill" list. "Give me that bag. I'm going to slice the shadow off that runner."

"Hey!" Blot snapped, yanking the bag back out of reach before the Dawn could grab it. "We don't *have* to help you."

Alan looked the man in the eye. "Listen to me," he said. "This is about saving lives. *All lives.* I'm fighting to keep you *and* them alive, because most of these Shades are conscripts who are as much a victim as the human they're dragging along with them. Is that clear? No shredding. You ward him off if you need to, but *no killing.* Now, I've got the directions to where your boss and the rest of the gear are located. If you can get me to the right spot, you get the gear and I get to return to see what I can do to keep the rest of the Dawn alive long enough for you to figure out how to reach them on a shut-down, half-flooded highway with downed power lines around it, got it? The route this van is liable to survive swings up to pretty much due west of the other van. That's the drop-off point for me. We'll surf the sun all the way back."

The man rumbled with restrained anger. "Get in," he growled.

"That's *right*," Blot jabbed, heaving the bag back into reality.

In the inexplicable white-and-gold monument to mystical knowledge, Jessie was grappling with the fact that she'd been so certain she wouldn't be able to *reach* this place that she didn't have a plan to find what she was after in the event that she did. In fairness, she had no idea what would be waiting for her. But a sprawling, vaulted hall that looked like it was some sort of eccentric, hyperreligious billionaire's personal museum was a fair distance down the list of expectations.

Jessie may have been lost, but she still had her intuition and her training. And in a place that was seemingly endless and pristine, filled with books and artifacts that her mind seemed to actively avoid perceiving, paradoxically the *mundane* was precisely the sort of thing that stuck out.

She reached the top of a staircase that led to the only dull and dim spot in the entire place. A bookcase filled with alarmingly unremarkable books was waiting for her. It had an assortment of children's literature, a full shelf of self-help books, some history and science textbooks, and a seemingly random assortment of magazines from the last seventy years. Beside it, three somewhat more arcane books had been set on stands, each open to a page with a diagram that moved and shimmered on the page as if alive.

A wheeled chalkboard stood behind the whole display, scrawled with what may have been a topological map, though it lacked any labels. The only distinctive parts of the map were glimmers of light and... glimmers of darkness? The light was amber colored, a fuzzy point of intensity, like a laser pointer without a source. The light was moving with the halting, not-quite-regular motion of a living thing viewed from overhead. The darkness was much fuzzier, and more spread out, a flashlight beam as opposed to a laser point, except it sapped light rather than shining it. This was a map tracking motion. This was how Angel "watched" them, precisely pinpointing humans and guessing at the positions of hidden Shades. She was sure of it. Something akin to the cone of a Victrola hooked over the top of the chalkboard, but if it was playing any sort of sound, Jessie couldn't hear it. Set on a table in front of those stands was a locked metal case matching the description she'd been given.

Jessie knew it couldn't be this easy, but there was nothing in her mental toolkit to call upon to prepare for whatever defenses the Glints might have in place. Her only plan, if it could be called that, was the tried-and-true tactic of first-time thieves since the dawn of time. She would grab it and run for all she was worth.

She was already coiling to launch into a sprint before she'd even fully grasped the case. The moment it was tucked under her arm, she launched toward the door. By her third stride, she felt a simmering warmth in the ring on her finger. By the fifth, she heard an unseen door opening. And by the tenth, she heard a voice.

"Stop," came Angel's exasperated demand.

Jessie's muscles locked midstride. She tumbled to the ground, unable to even straighten her legs to keep her balance.

Angel stomped up to her and fumbled with a pair of thick leather gloves. "Honestly. I don't know what to say," they said.

The phrase seemed like a soft one, but it was tinged with the confusion and fear of someone who had literally *never* not known what to say.

"You shouldn't have been able to get in here," they said. Angel carefully grasped the case. "Release it," they instructed.

Jessie did so. They turned the box about in place.

"At least you weren't foolish enough to try to open it. I wouldn't put it past the kind of person who would trifle with things of such corrosive power to do something as dangerous as attempting to steal the shard out of the case and use the empty case as some manner of decoy. You really can't be trusted with..." Angel trailed off. "Where is the other one?"

"I don't know," Jessie breathed.

"Get on your feet and tell me what you meant to do by coming to this place!"

Jessie stood and tried to look defiant even as she did precisely as instructed. "I came here to take a weapon away from you before you could use it to kill another swath of Shades and humans."

"I imagine you speak of the Burning Light. Why are you people so frightened of us? We only seek balance! And in what way is balance achieved or maintained by such an act? We would never, *could* never use such a heinous weapon. A weapon, in case you didn't know, that was originally crafted by the Shades to punish their own. I unlocked the secret of the Burning Light only a few hours ago, using, in part, research from the Dawn. And I did it so that we would understand the nature of the weapons which might be used against our world *and* yours. ... I mean just your world. I mean just *our* world. Because I am, of course, a human."

"Tell me this. Do you watch the others? Dina and Gabriel?" Jessie asked.

"Of course not. Our resources are far too limited to keep surveillance on one another."

"Check on them now. Check if they have the missing shard."

"I do not take orders from thieves," Angel stated.

"I wish I could say the same, but apparently I can't *help* but follow the orders you and the others give me."

"They are for your own good."

"I refuse to believe that even *you* are fooled by talk like that. I think you're afraid. Afraid to look yourself in the face. Afraid to look your superiors in the face."

"I will not be manipulated by such words."

"Prove you aren't afraid. Prove you actually care about the truth. Do whatever it is you do to spy upon the world and see if Dina and Gabriel have the shard. And while you're at it, see what they've *done*," Jessie said.

Angel stared intensely at her. Jessie could feel the pressure of their gaze in the back of her mind. A few more moments and she feared they'd force her very memories out of her head. A deft motion of Angel's hand flipped open the cover of a small pad that she'd not noticed them holding before. They turned to the page, giving Jessie the blessed relief of no longer being the focus of their attention.

Slowly Angel's neutral expression hardened. "Gabriel carries a shard..." they uttered. "It is drained. It has been used."

"Now see if anything's happened in Buffalo that might explain how it *became* drained."

Angel shuddered, but flipped the page. "The land is stained. Stained by the very magic I'd unlocked..."

"It hurts to know you've been used to hurt someone, doesn't it?" Jessie said.

Angel didn't answer. They just looked numbly at the locked case in their gloved hand.

"Now you know the truth," Jessie said.

Again, for a time, there was silence.

"We were supposed to stay distant. To act only sparingly, and only to restore balance. This... what was done... perhaps Dina and Gabriel truly believe what they did was necessary. Perhaps they believe it was restorative to the balance. But it was *not* sparing. It was *not* subtle. We have thrown a weight onto the scales larger than I've been taught to accept. And if we ourselves can upset the balance, then we must be a part of the equation to restore it." They looked at Jessie. "Follow."

She paced behind Angel as they approached the table that had formerly held the shard case. "What are you going to do?"

"Avert your eyes," Angel said.

Jessie turned aside. In the corner of her vision, she could see a deep violet gleam and the glitter of polished metal. A soft click snuffed the violet glow.

"Here. Take it," Angel said, handing her a silver locket. "I do not care for the state of the balance while it remains in my grasp."

She took it by the chain. Jessie had no concept of magic. Until very recently she hadn't even believed it existed. And she certainly had no desire or intention to learn it. But holding the chain of this barely imprisoned mystic gem felt... *real*. Like until now she'd just been skimming across the surface of the ocean, and now she'd been given a glimpse of how deep the waters truly were.

"Aren't you going to give me my marching orders?" Jessie said, carefully wrapping the chain and sliding the locket into her pocket.

"I do not know what to tell you to do, but I cannot say that I don't *care*. I want this set right. But clearly I cannot be trusted to decide what is right anymore. Not after what Gabriel and Dina have done. So take it. Do what *you* think is right. Perhaps, by taking from our power and adding to yours, things will tip in the right direction. Now go. Walk to the door and shut it behind you. You've given me the pain of realization. That's quite enough for one day. Walk away. Step back into the hallway. Do as your heart and mind tell you. But make your decisions well. And stay safe. Dina and Gabriel will need someone to run our Shade-related errands. I need to get my tools. It seems you've broken my door."

She turned and descended the stairs. Though she was doing as she was told, something felt different now. Perhaps Angel hadn't layered onto their words the power that made them irresistible. Perhaps holding the shard served as a measure of protection. But still, she walked, eager to be free of this place and hopeful that she could somehow persuade herself to forget what she'd seen here. There were powers far too potent to be trifled with. Simple survival instinct carefully whispered instructions, suggesting she never return to this place again, never even *think* about this place again.

But that was not the only voice in her mind.

Angel's words were looping through her thoughts. She'd spoken to countless criminals and suspects. Some were innocent, some were guilty, and she told herself that she'd never put away someone innocent. But regardless, there was a tone of voice someone used when speaking of their wrongs. All but the utter sociopaths had a flicker of shame in their words when they spoke of their crimes. Even when denying them, there was the sense that a part of them prayed for punishment, that the sting of getting away with an unjust act would take a larger toll on their minds than the punishment would. Even those who truly lacked shame or guilt betrayed themselves. There was an emptiness behind their eyes, a hollowness to their voice. It wasn't that they failed to feel guilt. It was that the part of them that *should* feel guilt just wasn't there. And for Angel, that kernel of guiltiness was intact, and not particularly well concealed. And something in what had been said was sticking in Jessie's mind. Bit by bit, fragments fell away, sifting the speech for its gem of hidden truth.

By the time she'd reached the door, just a few words were stuck on repeat in her mind.

"Stay safe," Jessie said, murmuring aloud. "Dina and Gabriel will need someone to run our Shade-related errands."

When the damaged door started to swing shut, the realization finally flashed into focus. She spun around and wedged her foot in the door before it could fully shut, then heaved it open. Angel was standing there, knocked back by her forced entry. They had the mildly scandalized look of someone who had never entertained the possibility that someone might physically accost them.

"Ms. Hearst, really. I—" Angel remarked.

She jabbed a finger in his face. "Officer Hearst! And what's happening to Alan right now?"

"Why would you think something was happening to him?"

"Because he's doing something *very* dangerous right now, which you *know*, and you pretty much just told me I was going to have to take over running *your* errands, which is the job you've given *him* right now. So tell me what's happening to him!"

"That isn't for you to—"

"I don't want to hear that! He's doing this because of *you*. Now *tell* me what you *know*!"

The Dawn van thundered along the street, swerving around slower vehicles and blasting through intersections with dead traffic lights. If the power outage and the chaos it had caused hadn't been keeping the police busy, they most certainly would have been surrounded and forced off the road.

But the same disaster that was threatening to wipe out several members of the Dawn and put their equipment back into Shade hands served to provide the perilously thin thread of a chance to rescue them.

"You're going to run out of road about two miles from the van," Alan said. "Traffic, emergency crews, news crews..."

"We'll manage."

"The angle of the sun is just about right. Are you ready?" Blot said.

"In a moment," Alan said. "Are you Dawn boys going to be able to turn the tide? There's only four of you."

"You worry about yourself," the driver said. "And don't get in our way."

"There's gratitude for you," Blot said. "Deep breath, Alan."

Alan nodded and took a breath. Blot yanked him into the shadows and was barely able to force herself through the windshield. But once she did, the sun breaking through the ragged edge of the storm hit them like an avalanche. She and Alan streaked across the city streets, sliding up walls and across roofs. They looped around trees and under cars. Alan wasn't even running short of his first breath when the highway came into view in the distance, and the dark clouds started to rob the light of its intensity and thus their journey of its breakneck speed.

"They're still alive," Blot said. "I can see the lights still shining."

An ear-splitting shriek echoed across the countryside. It wasn't the sound of a rikt being injured. It was the sound of a rikt warning just what sort of injuries it could cause.

"*And Chu-chu is still all right!*" Blot squealed happily. "A few more seconds and we'll be back to protect those ungrateful Dawn people. They better have something better than a truce to reward us with when this is over. We deserve a *parade* for what we're doing."

Alan tried to train his distorted gaze on the glow in the distance. It wasn't hard to spot. Flashing lights and sirens had gathered on either side of the battleground. What looked like half the police and firefighters in the state had arrived, but the fallen transmission towers still kept them from the van.

The rain was falling in sheets now, the dark clouds having thickened until they cast near-midnight darkness upon the highway. Alan gave Blot's arm a pat, signaling for a breath of fresh air.

"In a moment. We're too close to the shifters. If we pop up now—"

A rustle of motion drew Alan's eyes to the trees that served as a lackluster sound barrier between the highway and the closest houses. A moment later, he felt an icy, punishing sensation in his abdomen, like a blunt stick was trying to burrow through him.

Their forward motion came to a sudden stop and Blot grunted in pain. For a moment, Alan's view from the shadows was blurred and difficult to focus. When he fought the pain aside, he realized he was staring up from the ground into a familiar face. It was Brink, wielding a silver-tipped walking stick like the one the old man used. He was pressing it hard, trying to force it through Alan and Blot.

"Finish them. *Finish them*," demanded Dun.

The fiendish Shade commanding Brink kept its distance. The silver tip of the stick was just as much a threat to him as to Blot.

For a few seconds, Blot tugged and yanked at Alan, twisting and dangling like a fish at the end of a line. Then, finally, she released him.

Alan emerged from the shadows with the stick pressing painfully into his sternum. Brink forced his weight down upon it, pressing with the intent to splinter Alan's rib cage. But for all the agony the torturous attack put him through, it also placed his flesh-and-blood body between the silver and Blot.

"Enough!" she roared, rising up from the shadows in as massive and monstrous a combat form as she could muster.

She slashed her claws at Brink. He raised the walking stick to block, skillfully parrying the blow, then shifted his weight and slashed at her with the stick. It thumped her hard and knocked a scattering of the gear she carried with her to the wet ground. Among the equipment was one of Alan's cameras and a massive Maglite. He rolled aside and snatched them up.

Dun's iron-hard claws closed around his flashlight hand. His knuckles creaked and popped under the pressure of the Shade's grip. Alan cried out and held down the burst mode of the camera, strobing the darkened patch with painful, disorienting light that launched the Shade back. Brink charged forward again, attempting to split Alan's skull with the tip of the stick. Blot pulled him out of range and lurked beside him, smoldering white eyes fierce and determined.

For a moment, all four combatants took time to try to recover. Alan couldn't get his fingers to obey him, unable to summon the strength or dexterity to press the button on the flashlight. He still held the camera, but if he wanted another burst of full-force flash, it would need a few more moments to charge.

"How can you do this, Brink?" Alan said. "How can you abandon your ideals to help the worst of the Shades?"

"Silence," Dun said. "Brink is the first to see the truth. That darkness is indomitable. That the rising sun is *not* an inevitability."

"You don't understand the game you are playing, Fontaine," Brink huffed. "I don't want to kill you, but I can't afford to have you and your Shade on the table any longer. You are a wild card, and the stakes are too high."

"Who is playing who?" Alan said. "Either Dun is too afraid to make his move when his enemy is at his mercy, or you've been feeding him lies about the strength of the Dawn."

"Treachery," Dun said, surging forward to slash at him.

He took another burst of photos. Only the first had the force of the external flash. The rest were the wimpy built-in flash. It was a flurry of jabs instead of the haymaker he'd been hoping for, but it was enough to stagger Dun. Rather than falling back to dodge, Alan rushed forward, shoulder-charging Brink in what he hoped would be an unexpected offensive. Brink neatly sidestepped and swung the walking stick. Blot yanked Alan's leg, causing him to fall face-first onto the wet ground in a graceless move that very likely spared him a direct blow to the head and a fractured skull. Blot grabbed the stick and wrenched it away. Brink dropped, pressing his knee to the back of Alan's neck, mashing his face into the mud and cutting off his air.

Alan sputtered and gurgled, desperately trying to raise his head. Every attempt at a breath just dragged more muck and grimy water into his mouth. The world was starting to feel cold, distant, and subdued. His chest heaved and burned.

"Alan! *Alan, I can't hold Dun off!*" Blot shrieked, her voice the one thing that remained loud and clear in his mind.

But Brink was too heavy. Too strong. And Alan had been pushing himself too hard. He just didn't have anything left.

Jessie stomped breathlessly to the chalkboard, a few steps ahead of Angel.

"I shouldn't be letting you see this. You should really—"

"Don't you *dare* give me any instructions right now. Just show me what you know."

Angel pointed to the board, indicating areas of light and shadow. "Here, the Dawn. Around them, Shades, as best as we can track them. No deaths on either side, though not for lack of trying. Some injured Shades. One very bloody Dawn member. More Dawn here, recently met by Alan. He abandoned them here, and right between them... yes... it's happening now."

He tapped a vague area of light and a vague area of darkness. "This is a very strong Shade and human. Probably Brink and Dun. A stronger, better-trained human than Alan, with a stronger, better-trained Shade than Blot. They are fighting. Alan will lose. I'm sorry. He's already fading."

"Do something."

"Cannot interfere."

"You do nothing *but* interfere! Do something! Help him!"

"Gabriel and Dina outrank me, and there are two of them. If they wanted this stopped, then they would be stopping it. But they *aren't* so—"

"So *you* have to!"

"Ms. Hearst, calm—"

She grabbed Angel by the overalls and pulled them face to face. "For the last time, I am *Officer* Hearst and I do *not* take orders from you. You act like letting suffering happen is neutral. You *can* do something and you aren't. Your hands are as bloody as Dun's and Brink's."

"Dina and Gabriel... if I do something then... once we start changing things, where does it stop?" Angel said. "What they did with the Burning Light was wrong. This is the same."

"It isn't! Alan and Blot are trying to do what's right! If there is an ounce of the humanity you claim to have in you, you will give him a *chance*!"

"A chance?" Angel said, eyes turning to the fading light on the board. They sighed. "You are about to learn why it is so important to do our work through others," Angel said.

They reached up and plucked a short blond hair from their head and pinched it between thumb and forefinger. It straightened and became radiant, like the filament of an old-fashioned lightbulb. With a deft motion, like throwing a dart, they flicked it toward the chalkboard...

Alan, through sheer desperation, had managed to fight his face aside and get a breath of air, but Brink had shifted his position with the grim efficiency of someone who had done this a thousand times before. The larger man's knee had pinched off the blood flow. Air or no air, the light was fading from Alan's eyes. Even the struggle and grunt of Blot, a sound from within his own mind, was becoming distant. But a second sensation was weaving through the fringe of his fading mind. It was a tingly, hair-raising, pins-and-needles sensation. And then... the end of the world.

The sound was nothing short of apocalyptic. His ears had still been ringing from the shorting of the high-tension wires, but this sound struck him like a physical blow to the ears for a fraction of an instant. Then it was swallowed by a subdued hiss. At the same time, he felt a savage jolt arc through his body. His muscles tightened. His back arched backward in agony. The shock to his system was dizzying, but revitalizing, like someone had splashed him with water to bring him around, but the water had been scalding instead of cold.

As the assault on his senses faded, his vision started to return, and he realized the knee was no longer on his throat. Fueled by raw adrenaline, he lurched to his feet and tried to make sense of his surroundings. It was still pouring rain, the clouds overhead were still unnaturally dark. But there was more light than there was before. A flickering, roiling orange light and a choking smoke. One of the scraggly trees of the noise break was in flames. It must have been struck by lightning. He turned away from the tree, to his shadow. Blot was there, but her eyes were narrow slits of white, fluttering slightly every few moments. She was unconscious, or as close to it as was possible for a Shade. Convinced she was not in immediate danger, he swept the rest of the overgrown strip of dirt between highway and city. Brink was there, just a few steps away. He was still reeling, and Dun was similarly incapacitated.

If his mind was more fully functional, he would have run. But today, the fight-or-flight reflex had selected fight. An attempt to dash at the traitorous member of the Dawn turned into more of a staggering stumble. But unprepared as he was, Brink was unable to withstand the attack of desperation. The pair tumbled backward, Alan on top as they splashed to the wet ground. Brink may have been the one with the combat training, but

Alan had primal fear and righteous vengeance fueling him. They turned him into a whirlwind of wheeling arms. He battered and bludgeoned the slowly recovering Brink, bloodying the man's nose and Alan's knuckles.

The hiss in his ears turned to a whistle, then a crackle and terrified cries Alan realized were his own. Brink managed one sluggish block, then raised a hand and caught Alan's wrist in a crushing grip. The other ham hock of a hand reached for Alan's throat. In that split second, having exhausted the instincts of his ancestors, Alan fell back on the other crucible of his limited martial expertise, the schoolyard.

He delivered a panicked, punishing knee to Brink's privates. The blow loosened the man's grip, and Alan rolled free, immediately earning a painful thump to the back when he landed on what turned out to be Brink's silver-tipped stick. He grabbed it and stumbled back to his feet, wielding it like a baseball bat.

"Listen to me," Alan shouted. "I'm trying to save your life. All of your lives! How can you do this?! How can you turn your back on the Dawn? On everything you believe in?"

Brink wavered. For all his size and training, he was an older man and had taken his share of the abuse. He blinked mud and rain from his eyes and, for the first time, noticed his Shade was unconscious. An unearthly clarity came to his face.

"Fontaine," he said. "There are things the Dawn doesn't know. I don't want anyone to die either. When I was taken, I tried to end my life, but they stopped me. They tortured me, tried to turn me to their cause. I feigned defeat. I hoped to find a way to end them from within. But in playing the part, I learned from them."

"Learned from the Shades?" Alan said.

"The Dawn *can* defeat them. They always have, and they can again. But I can't let that happen. There is a greater foe. A foe the Dawn can't fight. A foe *no* human can fight. I've been trying to disarm the Dawn to protect the Shades because we need them alive. They're the lesser of two evils."

"The Glints. You're talking about the Glints," Alan said.

"You know of them..." Brink said.

Brink's gaze snapped to the ground. Dun started to stir. He looked back at Alan.

"Listen to me. Someone learned something. Discovered something. It happened between the last eclipse and this one. The Shades figured it out first, but the Glints aren't far behind. This time isn't like the others. We can't let the Shades fall. Even if it costs us the Dawn. Learn where I came from. Learn what was forgotten."

In the distance, crunching footsteps approached. The figures of the members of the Dawn, having worked their way to the city side of the wooded stretch, could be seen working their way closer.

"What happened..." Dun wheezed.

"They... have a weapon," Brink said quickly. "Something more dangerous to you than to me. And reinforcements are on the way. I warned you the Dawn wouldn't be so easily trounced."

"If I want your tactical advice, I will pry it from you," Dun hissed.

As much as Dun wished to appear in control, he was plainly left frightened and unsteady by the effect of the bolt of lightning. He mustn't have relished the thought of facing a second attack like that on the off chance the Dawn truly controlled a weapon that could hit so hard.

"Fall back. We will regroup," Dun demanded, his voice labored but booming.

A shaky claw rose from the darkness and pulled Brink into the shadows. Shades and hosts started to rush among the trees. The stronger of them or those farther from the lightning strike still had the strength to pull their hosts into the shadows. Others berated their dizzied and frightened hosts to run. But soon the attacking force had fully retreated. Seconds later, Chu-chu returned to them, burying himself in Alan's pocket to wrap about the stone. There was an uncharacteristic fear in the thing's motion. A moment later the Dawn reinforcement from the city and those led by the old man converged at the base of the burning tree.

"If you could pull a stunt like that, why didn't you do it in the *first place*?" the old man said.

"I didn't. It wasn't me," Alan said. "It was just lightning."

"Like hell it was," he said. "If the exploding wires didn't hit them that hard, the lightning shouldn't have. That bolt wasn't natural, it was supernatural. But keep your secrets, if that's how you want it." He turned to the reinforcements. "Lead us to your van. There's too many cops responding to those downed wires. A couple duffel bags of knives are liable to raise some questions we can't answer. Let's get out of here. Fontaine, I suggest you do the same."

"Right... Right... Blot, any chance you can get us back to the car?" he said.

"Ugh... Mmm... What?" she murmured thickly.

He released a sigh that turned into a groan and held a spot on his side where a bruise was rapidly forming. "All right... Long wet walk... But I'm alive." He sloshed along the muddy ground. "We're all alive. ... We made it..."

EPILOGUE

A lan shifted uncomfortably in his seat, hoping the dim light of Dr. Ling's office was hiding the visible consequences of his many inadvisable exploits. He'd only had three days to heal, and the throbbing welt on his chest was reminding him that it wasn't nearly enough to get him back in fighting shape.

"So. How have you been holding up?" Dr. Ling said.

"Oh, you know. Same ol' same ol'," Alan said.

"That's nice, Alan, but I'll remind you that you're paying me by the hour. We are here to help you, not make small talk."

"She's getting snippy. I knew the niceness was a mask," Blot said, suppressing a yawn.

That the Shade was incorporeal and didn't require sleep and yet was yawning underscored just how much effort she'd expended in the past week.

"How did you spend the week? Anything you'd like to discuss?" she said.

Alan shut his eyes, searching for something, anything, from the last few days that would make for good fodder for discussion. He'd learned from experience, and from Blot spying on her notebook, that Dr. Ling was almost unsettlingly capable of differentiating completely fabricated anecdotes from lightly massaged ones. She seemed willing to accept when Alan was leaving out key details about reality, but whenever he just outright made things up or listened to Blot's suggestions, the doctor would tug at the threads to cause the story to unravel, then gently ask if he had anything else he wanted to discuss. But there really wasn't much that wouldn't sound like utter lunacy.

"I... had a nice meal with Jessie at the diner," Alan said.

That much had been true... for certain values of nice.

Two days prior...

For once, when Alan walked through the door of the diner, Jessie was already there. She'd made sure that there were three coffees waiting on the table, and she was buttering a roll from the complimentary basket. A glance at her shadow revealed the ever-present Frightful, who was probably the reason for the half-empty plate of sausage on the table.

"Are you all right? You look really beat-up," Jessie said, face scrunched up in concern.

"You should see the other guy," Alan said.

"The other guy looks much better," Blot grumbled.

As Alan slid into the booth, Jessie handed him a menu.

"Honey's on shift," Jessie said. "She's eager for a chat."

"I'm starting to wonder if she's ever *not* on shift," Alan said.

He flipped open the menu. As he looked it over without actually reading it—he'd eaten here far too many times to have to rely upon a menu to know what he wanted—a soft clicking noise drew his attention to Jessie's hand. She was tapping her silver ring against the side of her coffee cup as she held it.

"It's surprisingly cool today," she said, conversationally.

Blot took the hint. She stuck a hand in Alan's pocket and dropped the silver pendant. He slipped his hand in and felt it. The silver was cool to the touch, as it had been since the day of the clash.

"So we're still not being watched," he said.

"I haven't felt a hint of warmth from this thing since the power outage you took all the pictures of," Jessie said.

"If we're talking openly about being watched by the Glints, we may as well talk openly about everything else," Blot said.

"That's true," Jessie said. "The point is, you'd think after what I did in particular, they would be breathing down our necks. But neither hide nor hair on my end."

"Mine either. Maybe they've picked new people to pick on."

"Or maybe they're too busy with Stigma," Blot offered. "Stigma *is* the leader of the shades, after all. The ones still doing what they came here to do, at least. After a strike like the one the white-suits managed against him, it wouldn't surprise me if he was three steps into a fifty-step plan to tear them to pieces and feed him to a rikt." She switched to a baby voice. "You'd probably like a piece, wouldn't you, Chu-chu?"

The little rikt squawked from inside Alan's pocket but didn't emerge.

"Aw... poor baby is still tired..." Blot said.

"We have to entertain the possibility Stigma is dead," Jessie said. "The death toll is up to seventeen from the Buffalo massacre, according to the news. Any one of them could have been Stigma, right?"

She spoke in a carefully moderated tone, but there was a tension on the words "Buffalo massacre" that did not go unnoticed.

"What happened in Buffalo wasn't your fault. You couldn't have known what might happen, and you can't be sure you could have stopped it even if you *did* know. The only reason you were able to take the other shard was because all the Glints were distracted. Who knows how you would have gotten in before that?"

"We can't be sure I *couldn't* have prevented it. I dragged my feet on getting my hands on the shards, and one of them was used to take thirty-four lives."

"Thirty-four," Alan said. "Humans *and* Shades..."

"If you're trying to get on my good side by including the Shades in your tally for the tragedy... you're on the right track," Blot said.

"I wasn't currying favor. I was being accurate. And the point is, because of Blot and Frightful, you and I have an awareness and a capacity that other people lack. Maybe it is true that I couldn't stop what happened. But it's certainly true that no one *else* could have. You and I have an obligation to do what we can to protect the people who can't perceive the threats that we can."

"We don't have an obligation," Blot said. "There's no cosmic rule maker handing out assignments."

"That's a matter of philosophical and theological debate, but we should *feel* like we have an obligation, at least," Jessie said. "I can claim ignorance for this one, but now my eyes are open to the stakes."

Honey stepped up to the table and cheerfully placed the doohickey down. "Been busy, huh?" she said once it was spinning.

"Very," Jessie said.

Alan pointed to the spinning contraption. "That might not be necessary. The Glints seem to have lost interest."

"Better safe than sorry," Honey said. "Did you do the enchantment stuff okay?"

"It depends on how you define 'okay,'" Alan said. "We didn't die."

"And did you get the shards?" Honey asked.

"One of them," Jessie said.

"There were supposed to be three at the sandwich shop, according to the Dawn. We only found two," Alan said.

"There were only two to *find*," Blot defended.

"And one of them is in the hands of the Glints and was used to commit a war crime," Jessie said.

"That thing in Buffalo?" Honey asked gravely.

Jessie nodded.

"I'm going to be watching the news very differently, now that I know what I know," Honey said.

"You and me both," Jessie said, reaching into her pocket. "So do I give this to you or..."

"No! No, no, no," Honey said quickly. "You're just carrying that thing around? Look, get rid of it, ASAP. I'm just a waitress. You give it to the Dusk proper as soon as you can."

"So, Gladys then?" Alan said.

"She'll do," Honey said.

"You'd be better at handling that than me," Jessie said, tossing the silver-encased shard to Alan. Blot intercepted it by snatching the shadow, then yanked it down and vanished it a little too eagerly.

Honey topped off all coffee cups within reach, then snatched the doohickey from the table, signaling the end of supernatural talk for the time being. "So, what can I get you two for your meal?" she said.

"Chop cheese," Alan said. "Lately I'm a lot less concerned about the long-term effects of my diet on my longevity. I feel like other factors are going to be the decision maker on if I reach old age."

"Egg-white omelet," Jessie said. "Feta cheese and spinach."

Honey jotted down the order and scurried off to have it filled.

"So," Alan said, placing Blot's coffee on the seat beside him so she could more easily partake. "What are the big concerns right now? I think I'm between errands from the various supernatural entities that have been running my life."

"I'd say those other shards of shadow are the top priority," Jessie said. "Especially the one that's in the hands of the Glints. We've seen what it can do, and we can't let them do that again."

"They probably can't do it again in a hurry," Blot said. "I'm not arguing with you. We *do* need to get it away from them. I'm very concerned about the fact they have it. But for now it's probably expended and will need to be restored over time. But if you think we *can* or *should* do something about them with the resources we have right now, you are mistaken. They have the Burning Light, and the 'protection' of our apartment is supplied by them. Not to mention, they seem to be able to travel from anywhere to anywhere instantly. If they want us dead, they can do it whenever they like. I'd really rather not have them remember that anytime soon. This is very much a 'heads down if we want to keep them' situation."

"That's another thing, though," Jessie said. "One of the survivors of the Buffalo massacre did so by traveling through some sort of tunnel that got them here in minutes. What is *that* about? And what do we do about it?"

"I don't know," Blot said. "I remember hearing about methods to move over great distances, but that was part of the endgame, so it was a long way away from the sort of stuff they were teaching me."

"The end game," Alan said. "As in, they are about to make some big, final move?"

"As in, they won't make a big, final move until it is in place. And it sounds like the Glints wrecked this one with the Burning Light."

"But that means some part of the Shade endgame involves Buffalo?" Jessie said.

"Maybe, maybe not," Blot said. "You need to think of things from a ritual point of view. Sometimes things can only happen in certain places. The eclipse could only have granted us access to your world through that very specific tree in that very specific field. That they opened a tunnel between Philadelphia and Buffalo means Philadelphia and Buffalo are currently mystically useful locations. That's about all we can be sure about."

"It seems like if we wanted to be sure about things, we'd have to—" Alan began.

His phone rang, making him practically jump out of his seat. He fumbled for it, half expecting to be receiving a call from the Glints, or the Shades, or the Dawn, or the Dusk. At this point, a call from the grim reaper telling him he was overdue for an appointment wouldn't have been out of place. As it turned out, it was Mr. Cox. Alan thumbed the answer button.

"Yes, Mr. Cox?" he said.

"If it isn't Disaster Boy," Cox said. "I hate to say it, because you might get a big head, but for the past two weeks, you've brought in about sixty percent of Cox Media's earnings."

"It's seventy-nine percent," Blot said. "I've seen the spreadsheet."

"You've been getting up close and personal with so many major regional events, I'd half expect to find out you're *causing* them. And how'd you pull off these paydays? By cutting out most of that pesky 'art' stuff and just going for the gut punch, like I've been telling you to do for years. Welcome to the money-making side of photojournalism, my boy. But listen. I've got people beating down my door for shots of the Black Bird of the Highway."

"The what?" Alan said, still stinging from being told abandoning art had been his secret to success.

"The Black Bird of the Highway! It's what the kids are calling the smear in some of these *other* photos that are circulating from that power-line collapse on the highway."

Alan glanced at Jessie, who was already tapping at her phone. In moments, she brought up a very blurry image. It had clearly been post-processed to lighten it up, but a highly distorted and heavily arti-facted image of Chu-chu in his battle form was just barely discernable in the center.

Alan shut his eyes tight. The only time that a non-Shade host could properly see a Shade was when it imposed itself on reality. Apparently, that went for rikts as well.

"I'm seeing a picture, yeah," Alan said.

"You were *right there* and you didn't get a shot of it?"

"It's probably an optical illusion," Alan said.

"*Of course* it's an optical illusion. It's probably a moose that got caught in the mud or something. Point is, I want a better shot of it. Not a *good* one. I don't want it looking clear enough for these cryptid fanatics to be able to see it's just a deer having a bad day, but go through your raw footage and see if you can find it. I know you artsy types hold back stuff you think doesn't show off your skill, even though it specifically says in your contract that I get *all memory cards*. So dig through and see if you find it. This has serious 'bigfoot' potential."

"I'll... take a look, sir..."

"You do that."

Cox hung up without saying goodbye. Alan lowered the phone.

"We're getting a little too sloppy," Blot said. "But I guess if we need some extra money, we can get Chu-chu to pose. Isn't that right, Chu-chu..."

"Let's focus," Alan said. "We don't know how long this little calm moment is going to last. We need a plan..."

"All in all, a nice visit," Alan said, completing an incredibly edited version of the account.

"Mmm..." Dr. Ling said, her tone supremely doubtful. "You know something, Alan. How these sessions go is entirely up to you, but I really think if you are more forthcoming, you'll feel better."

"I'm being as forthcoming as I can," Alan said.

"All right. I won't push," Ling said. "Any highlights?"

"Highlights?" he said.

"Yes! Any career achievements, perhaps? You've spoken about how important your art is to you, and your new position at the police department."

"Career achievements..." Alan said.

"She's not going to stop picking until we give her something. She always gets nosy when you don't give enough details. Listen up. This is what you did this week..."

Blot started to spin a yarn, but the words just washed over Alan as he stared into the middle distance, each second increasing the clarity of his impossible position. His brain felt raw. He'd been doing nothing but thinking about what he could do, what he should do. What he needed to do. He'd been thinking about the risks he was taking by action and opposing risks of inaction. He felt his heart racing even now, like he was actively being pursued. He needed help. And he was in the office of someone who *should* be able to provide it for him. But instead of getting that help, he was just tying himself in further knots, trying to keep her from finding out the truth of his problems while desperately trying to sweep together the crumbs of advice and relief he could allow himself to get.

He was tired. He was tired of hiding. Tired of turning away the help he needed.

"... and as a result, you're perfectly happy and she's cured you so you can cancel any future appointments," Blot finished. "Say it."

"It was a fairly average week," Alan said woodenly. "I got down to Baltimore for a crab festival."

"Don't tell her the *truth*!" Blot yelped.

"The crab festival? You were lucky you didn't get caught up in that riot."

"Nope."

Blot physically slapped the back of his ankle. "You're doing this on purpose. Snap out of it," she growled.

"Nope? Do you mean to say you *didn't* avoid the riot?"

"Yep. Got a lot of good pictures of it, too. Those were probably the ones you saw on the news."

"And you didn't feel as though that was worthy of note?"

"I *said* same ol' same ol'," he said.

She raised her eyebrows. "You mean to suggest that you regularly become involved in such things?"

"That's the job. Gotta get the good pictures."

"Alan, you're going to get *so* many questions for this," Blot said. "Why are you saying these things?"

"Alan, if you're being honest, I'm concerned you're attempting to use dissociation as a further coping mechanism. More pressing, if you truly consider involvement in a spontaneous instance of public violence to be unworthy of note, then you may be engaging in purposely self-destructive acts."

"Yeah, probably."

"*Alan...*" Blot fumed.

"That is a significant red flag, Alan," Dr. Ling said.

"You're going to get us locked up. Do you *want* to get us locked up?" Blot said.

"It may be wise to consider voluntary admission for psychiatric evaluation," the therapist said.

"*See?!*" Blot barked. "How do you think things will go if you're locked up and Dun or Stigma decide it's time to take us out?"

"If you need recommendations"—Dr. Ling reached for a drawer—"I can give you some names of some very—"

"Hold on," Alan said. "Blot's yelling at me."

"*DON'T SAY MY NAME!!!*" Blot screeched. "You're not supposed to refer to me at *all*!"

Dr. Ling hastily abandoned the drawer and flipped to a clean page in her notebook. "Blot. And that would be the name you've applied to your darker impulses."

"You're doing this on purpose now, I know it," Blot said. "This is not okay. This is going to have consequences, Alan."

"Let me ask you this, Doctor," Alan said. "We've got that doctor-patient privilege, right? Nothing leaves this room?"

"Confidentiality, not privilege. And yes, within reason, of course," she said.

"Not a whole lot of reason in my life right now, Doc. I'm going to need a straighter answer than that."

"Short of rare legal exceptions, your words are between you and me."

"Alan, whatever you're thinking, stop thinking it," Blot said.

He looked Dr. Ling in the eye. "One moment."

He looked down. "Blot. I'm at the end of my rope. We're in the middle of something I don't see the end of. If she can help give me some sort of guidance, *something* to hold me together, I desperately need it. I don't know if I can get the help I really need if she doesn't know the truth about you, because the way we've been doing it is definitely messing with the diagnosis."

Blot glanced at Dr. Ling, who was feverishly taking notes. "Think about this for a second, Alan. This could go really wrong for us if she doesn't handle this right."

"I wouldn't call how it's going right now *good*."

"We're alive, aren't we?"

"I'd like to aim higher than that." He looked at Dr. Ling again, then back at Blot. "It's up to you."

"That's right. It *is* up to me. Because you're not convincing her without me actually cooperating. I could *not do* anything, and then she'd have you locked up for talking to your shadow, and then I'd bust you out, and we'd be fugitives, and you'd *owe me*."

"Alan," Dr. Ling said. "I think you need to accept that there won't be any answers like this. Your shadow can't help you."

Blot sighed. "Tell her to promise she won't scream," she grumbled.

"Blot asks you to brace yourself and not shout," Alan said.

"I will be entirely professional, as I have always been," Dr. Ling said. "What do you have to show me?"

Blot gritted her nonexistent teeth. "I'm saying it one more time. This is a bad idea. But so be it."

She slid beneath the chair, disappearing behind it. Gradually, she eased her way up and teased her hands out of the darkness to grip the back of the seat. She started to ease herself out of the shadows with the sort of labored effort that suggested she wouldn't be doing her combat form for a while, and she emerged. She reached around the side of the chair once she'd reached the full, albeit diminutive, height of her impish form. She held tight to the arm of the chair and moved like a first-time ice skater trying to remain upright. She turned her milk-white eyes to Dr. Ling. The therapist was wide-eyed. Her fingers were clutching her pad so tight it was curling in her grip. The cap of her pen popped off and bounced to the ground.

"This... is very... irregular," the therapist said, her voice hushed.

"You're going to want to order more pens, Doctor," Blot said. "And would it kill you to get some legal-size clipboards?" She pointed. "You're ruining your pad."

"Well, Doc? See why I've been 'evasive' until now?" Alan said.

"It was... perhaps... justified..." Dr. Ling said.

"Uh-huh. So maybe *now* you'll quit trying to get rid of his 'dark side' and just untie his brain knots so we can focus on what's *important*," Blot said.

"Right. Yes." She cleared her throat. "Mr. Fontaine, I think that will be enough for today. We'll discuss this next time."

"Remember," Blot warned. "Doctor-patient confidentiality, or whatever."

The Shade released her grip and dropped back into the shadows. Alan stood up.

"Sorry, Doc. I just needed to set the record straight."

"It is best that you did, Alan." She gazed at his shadow, which from her point of view, once again appeared mundane. "We might want to skip the next session. I need to... reassess some of my prior findings. All of them, in fact."

"Yeah," Alan said, heading for the door. "Blot has a way of making you reassess a lot of things. But she'll win you over."

From The Author

Thank you for reading! If you liked this story, or perhaps if you found it lacking, I'd love to hear from you. You can find me online at my website, bookofdeacon.com. For **free stories** and important updates, join my newsletter.

Discover Other Titles by Joseph R. Lallo

The Book of Deacon – an Epic Fantasy Series:

Book 1: *The Book of Deacon*
Book 2: *The Great Convergence*
Book 3: *The Battle of Verril*
Book 4: *The D'Karon Apprentice*
Book 5: *The Crescents*
Book 6: *The Coin of Kenvard*
Book of Deacon Anthology: Volume 1
Book of Deacon Anthology: Volume 2

Other stories in the same setting:

The Rise of the Red Shadow
The Story of Sorrel

Entwell Origins: Anya
The Redemption of Desmeres
The Adventures of Rustle and Eddy
Jade
Halifax
The Stump and the Spire

The Big Sigma Series – a Sci-fi/Space Opera Series:

Book 1: *Bypass Gemini*
Book 2: *Unstable Prototypes*
Book 3: *Artificial Evolution*
Book 4: *Temporal Contingency*
Book 5: *Indra Station*
Book 6: *Nova Igniter*
Book 7: *Quantum Shift*
Beta Testers
Big Sigma Collection: Volume 1
Big Sigma Collection: Volume 2

The Free-Wrench – Steampunk Adventure Series:

Book 1: *Free-Wrench*
Book 2: *Skykeep*
Book 3: *Ichor Well*
Book 4: *The Calderan Problem*
Book 5: *Cipher Hill*
Book 6: *Contaminant Six*

Milton Keynes UK
Ingram Content Group UK Ltd.
UKHW041736231124
451587UK00027B/80

9 781631 070716